23:27

23:27

H. L. ROBERTS

CADAVA PUBLISHING

For Ashley–

May your dreams, memories, and soul always rest in peace.

H xx

PROLOGUE

TIME.

In the beginning, that was all there was. Seconds, minutes, hours pressed together, forming a mask of illusion that could never be dropped. A wall of steel grew around their hearts, one that couldn't be broken. The United Misfits image could never be distorted.

It was wrong. It wasn't right. No matter what her heart told her, it was wrong. Every flutter that skated through her stomach. His every skipped heartbeat, meant nothing. She was nothing. He was nothing. They were nothing.

It had been said many times, by many different people, the most broken person in the world could hide behind a perfected smile and a fake laugh. This could carry out a person's persona, something that never even existed to begin with. That would never exist. Laughter and smiles filled with fake truths and real lies could hide what that person wanted to show, or to tell, the truth.

In the end, she wanted to break free, but chains restrained her, blocking each move before she could make a single one, turning her into a prisoner, a captive in her own life.

Those chains squeezed tighter and tighter, never loosening their grip. They choked her from the inside, wrapping her tighter with every deceitful accusation and fake persona *they* put in her life. Deadly thoughts clouded her vision and stomped through her mind. Both of their minds.

Their hearts were noosed, yanked in every which direction. Like a snake. Until it all stopped. Until they both stopped fighting.

And when the fight dissipated, she could no longer turn away from the deceitful ways they had so graciously bestowed on her.

Chapter 1

Lilith

THAT WAS IT. The final straw that made me snap. I knew I couldn't take it anymore. Everything that happened this afternoon was the last push I needed to get me right over the edge. The last push I needed to make me break. *It was done.*

I was done.

I could feel it eating away at me, clawing its way into every fiber of my body, mind, and soul, searching for something to reach out and hold onto and never let go. My mind spun so fast I couldn't keep up, and more importantly, I couldn't place the emotion. What was it? Guilt? Maybe. Shame? Probably. Longing? Most likely. Love? Definitely.

Stupid love.

Why couldn't I just forget it and move on? Everyone else could. *He did. My band did.* But I couldn't. I continued to hold onto that one little thing. Something that would *never* happen; something that *could* never happen. *Why?* Because it was wrong. *Wrong in their eyes.* It would send the fans into a riot. It would break the band up. It would be the end of everything we had worked so hard for. Although, I couldn't because I'd never known anything that made my heart pound quite so much. Beautiful. What we had. It could only be described as beautiful. Together, we could be better. So much better. But, no. He forgot. Like they did. He moved on. Like everyone else had. But, not me. I couldn't. I never would.

I stayed behind, lurking in the shadows of the past— *our past.* The past of something that held a future that was never meant to be. We had made plans. But now, almost eighteen months down the road, those plans were long forgotten. Thrown into the fire, turned to ashes. Just like my heart. But I did not forget Alec. Not now. Not ever.

I walked past the small silver mailboxes that lined the walls in the entranceway to my apartment building and slowly climbed the staircase to my apartment. Peace and privacy awaited me there, and I craved it more than I cared to admit. I could not bear for anyone to look at me right now. My dreams and thoughts would shine back at them and that, more than anything, caused my heart to still in my chest. If anyone saw...if I let them...I couldn't bear to continue. With what I was planning... no, I couldn't risk it. In the end, they would always try to stop me, not because they care about me but because they cared about the money I make for them. So, this was the only way, my only chance.

I unlocked the door to my small hideaway, my apartment and walked inside, pausing to take in the sameness of everything.

However, as I turned on the lights, I took in every small detail, tucking it inside my memory along with everything else that had happened here. A faint smile spread across my lips as I walked through the living room, memories crashing through my mind like a whirlwind—the pillow fights and the pretend wrestling matches. He would always let me win. The tickling wars that I lost every time because I would be laughing too hard to do much else. The late-night conversations that passed throughout the night without us even noticing.

The living room had always been my favorite room in the whole apartment. It held so many secrets—the secret movie nights, the popcorn fights that accompanied them, and the sleepovers that followed. Lying next to each other, we'd share our secrets—but not our deepest ones—well, at least, not mine.

I stepped to the bookshelf, eyeing the pictures lining the shelves. Some from my childhood, to the best days of my life with the band, all the memories captured onto these small bits of paper that I now keep all for myself. My favorite picture caught my eye, the one they took right after they picked me as lead singer. It was the same day I met them—well, most of them. I had met Chloe-Grace earlier that week. She introduced me to her older brother Jaxson and his two best friends, fraternal twin brothers Jase and Alec, after my first full week at the new school in Indiana. A week later, we figured out we weren't half bad together. That was when everything started to change for us.

We recorded videos, uploading them to YouTube. We performed gigs at every opportunity. It was six months later when our luck soared. We had a talent scout approach us after winning a local talent show, wanting to introduce us to Star Records and Management.

As I continued to move my eyes, I took in the subsequent pictures to see more of the monumental moments we had in our career. They showed everything that happened to us over the years, from winning our first Billboard award to performing at the Grammy's, not to mention when we got the opportunity to perform at the infamous Madison Square Garden. The pictures made me smile a little because of the small talks and the deep conversations hidden within them, the ones I would never forget.

I quickly shook those thoughts from my head and continued toward my bedroom, ignoring the rest of the apartment and focusing on my destination. Keeping my eyes glued to the door, I hid a black bag in the closet. I moved on to what I needed to pack. My diary, which I had written in every day since we started the band. My mom had told me once that one day, when this was all over, I would want something to remember each moment, both the good and bad. I grabbed my photo album, each picture in it holding a special meaning, a secret message. Lastly, I grabbed my laptop, stuffing it in the bag along with my other precious items, secrets, and hidden stories.

I paused in the doorway, turning back one last time to take one more look around. Memories slammed into me so hard I closed my eyes—laughter and stolen soft kisses, every one leading to the love we couldn't have fought if we wanted to. So much love I could barely let my mind wander there without my heart threatening to melt from my chest into a puddle at my feet.

"It's for the best," I whispered to the room, before bending and picking up the bag by the door. With tears falling, I kept my eyes trained on my shoes and let my feet do the walking to the front of my small apartment.

As I turned the knob on my front door, my mask fell into place, erasing every feeling from my face like I'd been taught. I became the fake persona—the person I'd never let myself become. Raising the hood of my black hoodie, I whispered to the apartment, knowing I would never be back.

"Goodbye, Alec."

***

19:15

I hastily made my way to my car, knowing how hard this would be. How hard it always was. I kept my head down, though that rarely helped. No matter what disguise I wore, the fans and paparazzi always saw right through it.

I tugged my hat and hood down a little further before sliding cheap, disposable sunglasses on. My eyes jolted around me, and not finding anyone nearby, I continued down the block to a cheap, rundown-looking car that I bought so I could get away when I wanted to. Since my other car had a GPS tracker in it, I knew better than to use it. I learned that one the hard way.

I grabbed a key from the pocket of my jeans and unlocked the car, which took longer than I wanted as my shaky fingers fumbled to find the keyhole. As I slid inside and shut the door, I locked myself inside in case someone saw me. I took a long, shuddering breath, refusing to let myself think about the things I'd be leaving behind. I couldn't because if I did...if I did, there'd be no way I'd follow through. I would cave like I had so many times before.

More than anything else, I was tired of this. Caving in. Conforming. Becoming the perfect image of what they wanted me to be all the time. It was exhausting. It was stupid. It put so much pressure on me, so much stress and it was all unneeded and unwanted. My life didn't need any more complications.

The traffic was busier than I expected it to be, not too difficult to get through but it took more time than I would have liked. I hated time. It made me think. Thinking made me hurt. Time made me hurt.

I laughed to myself about how they had made the world see me. A daredevil, a wild child, a ride-or-die chick, a rebel, a girl who was always down for a practical joke. A long time ago I could have been her, but not now. No, now I was a liar, a fraud, depressed, unhappy, fake, nothing. Yes, I had become nothing to them.

The world saw me as the glue to the band. The girl who held everything together with my practical jokes, my daredevil tendencies, and my outrageously outgoing personality. At least in public. They'd decided I needed to act the part, so my face had changed. Every day for the past four years, I'd pasted on that face. But it was fake. My big fake persona.

Every day since, I'd lost a little bit more of myself, leaving only a shell filled with so much unhappiness, some days I couldn't breathe. Every day since I signed the contract.

All the excitement and drive I had for the band died the day they took everything away from me, the same day they threw this fake life at me and forced me to accept it. I never asked for it. However, they all knew the only thing we were to the world, and most importantly to Star Records, was a product. Whether the band stayed together or split apart, they would make sure we sold records. They only cared about money. And I hated it.

To be an object of adoration, something to make them oodles of money, became the one thing I hated more than anything. It used to be about loving what I did, but things changed so fast I couldn't remember when I'd stopped. They wanted people to believe dreams could come true. They wanted people to gasp and point and cause scenes. So, we became actors and the people, and the fans bought it. It tore my heart out knowing the people would never know who I was because Star Records and Management turned me into a stranger even I didn't know.

When I drove up to my destination, a rundown motel, I kept my sunglasses on, in case someone recognized me. Once I parked my car, I tugged my bag from the backseat and hopped out, entering through a door with chipped green paint.

A teen sat behind the desk quickly texting away at whoever was at the other end (*probably her friends*) loudly popping a piece of gum and looked at me with no recognition at all on her face. Good.

"Room for one?" she asked.

I nodded in reply.

"How long?" she asked, minimizing her words. She typed something into her computer without a second glance at me.

Perfect.

"One night, please," I hurriedly replied. After all, that was all the time I needed. I was afraid I might have responded too quickly, but the teenager didn't notice anything. Good. I didn't need anyone to be alerted until it was too late. She asked me basic information for the room; my name, age, and to take a photocopy of my ID. After I gave her my fake name, age, and, of course, my fake ID, I paid in cash. She handed me the key.

"You're on the third floor; it's the second to last door on the right side. Have a good night." With that, the girl got up and disappeared through a door to what looked like an office.

I watched for a minute before turning the opposite direction and walking into the elevator. It smelled musty and stale as the doors clanked shut and I pressed the button to my floor. My chest felt heavy, and I froze as the elevator hovered for several seconds, making me think it didn't work and I might die of suffocation in this thing, but then it shot up making me wrap my arms around my stomach. I chuckled to myself. When the doors opened, I wasted no time, stepping out into a dreary hallway and making my way toward my room.

The small room was dimly lit, and my arms broke out in goose bumps from the cold. A smile stretched across my face. It was perfect. I hung the "do not disturb" tag on the knob and shut the door, locking it behind me. I walked a little further in and took a seat on the full-sized bed, throwing my hat off before pulling my hoodie up over my head. I unwrapped the hair tie from my long blonde and pink hair, letting it fall from the tight bun onto my shoulders. Then I looked around at the room, taking in every detail. A small lump formed in my throat, exactly like I knew it would. The room looked exactly like the other room *we* had stayed in two years ago. Same colored walls. The same type of furniture set up. Even the same bedding. What a coincidence.

I took a deep, shaky breath. Even though it sounded crazy, I could almost hear the echoes of our laughter tangled together, just like our bodies. Our playful banter and kisses that always started slow but turned into a fiery passion burning through every part of me.

***

3 years ago

"Lil, come back to bed," he whispered to me as I walked back in the room with breakfast.

"No, you lazy goon! Now get out of bed, it's time to eat..." I laughed, letting the bag sit on the table before turning to look at him.

To me, he was amazing. Beautiful. Everyone always fell in love with his wild hair, dark mysterious looking eyes, or even the smirk permanently plastered on his face, but not me. No, I fell in love with his nose, which always made me laugh. It sounded so stupid but every time I planted a light kiss on the tip of his nose, he would wrinkle it in return and bat me away with a laugh, telling me to stop. I never did.

"But, babe. I can think of much better things to do with our time than eat," he said with that ever so insightful smirk of his.

"Well, if you want to have the energy to continue that, then you'll let me eat." I chuckled. He rolled his eyes and sighed.

"Fine," he said, lifting himself out of bed. "But, I'm not getting dressed."

"I wouldn't want you to," I replied with a smile, pulling the food out of the bag. Creeping up behind me, he wrapped his arms around my waist and placed his chin in the crack between my neck and shoulder.

"Can we stay like this forever, Lil?"

His breath tickled my ear and I angled back, looking into his eyes. "What do you mean?" I softly questioned, trying not to get distracted by his fingers making soothing circles along my hips.

"This—us." He smiled softly, "I never want this to end. What we have is something I never want to lose, and I love you too much for that to happen."

My heart melted every time he said things like that. It never got old. I nodded my head, unable to speak, and leaned up to press a kiss against his cheek.

I paused, swallowing around the lump in my throat. It took a minute to compose myself, but when I did, I whispered, "I love you too. This, our love, is something that will never be lost."

If only I had known exactly how empty his promise was.

***

I shuddered, the cold in the room snaking over me as I blinked the memories away. Every time I let my mind drift back to those moments, the good times, the ever-growing hole in my heart grew bigger and bigger. Black edges already lined my soul, but those lines thickened with every happy memory. I couldn't stop them, but I wanted to. More than anything. If only I could find a way to forget the good days. Then maybe the bad days wouldn't seem so bad.

But, I couldn't.

Sighing, I slowly stood and pulled the bag open before turning it upside down, spilling the contents onto the bed. I changed clothes, pulling on a pair of dark-colored skinny jeans, a white tank top, and black high tops. Finally, I pulled on an oversized Rolling Stones concert tee. But it didn't belong to me. It was his. Even though I told myself otherwise, I needed this. A little piece of him with me, by my side until the very end.

Just like that promise.

I tossed my dirty clothes into a pile on the floor, not caring where they landed and sat down on the bed. I looked at the items surrounding me and picked up the photo album.

As soon as I opened it, a smile I couldn't stop lined my lips. The picture of my parents and me looking like ants in front of the Statue of Liberty caused a pang to shoot across my chest. They were probably the most important people to me when it came down to it because they had always been there for me in some way. I hadn't even gone one day without contacting them, until recently. Sometimes I called my mom and texted my dad, or vice-versa. On the weekends, we Skyped together. My crazy schedule with interviews, working on the next album, award shows, or concerts made keeping in touch difficult, but I always found a way.

As I looked at all the pictures of my mom and me, I remembered everything she'd done for me. For *us*. She fought so hard for Alec and me to be together. My love for my mom grew a hundred times larger in those moments alone. But in the end, even her fight couldn't change anything. Although, it did give me even more respect for the woman who brought me into this world.

"I am going to miss you s-so m-much," I whispered as a single tear plopped onto the photo, only one thought slinking through my mind.

Part of me wants to die tonight, part of me wants it to end in an accident, and part of me wants someone to notice and find me. But that wasn't going to happen because I won't let it happen.

Chapter 2

Lilith

Four Years Ago

WE HAD FINISHED another long day of boring meetings and interviews. Well, I shouldn't call them boring. We were working on our dream career, after all. But eight hours in a room full of dull old men in suits had worn us down. Of course, these meetings were all important ones, like working on the recording schedule and writing our first album. Up until now, we'd never even seen the inside of a real recording studio. We were all beyond excited about this, finally putting the final pieces together on our first album and getting ready to start the recording process. We were more than thrilled.

Jaxson, Jase, Alec, CG, and I made our way out of the tall office building we'd been stuck in all day to a black van waiting out front. I fell into the back seat, and my eyes drifted shut immediately. But, they snapped open when someone brushed up against my knees. I glanced over to see an overly excited Alec. The three guys were the oldest and the original members of our band and had wanted this for much longer than any of them would care to admit.

While I could say, the never-ending questions got to me; he remained enthusiastic about them. He was willing to go along with anything they threw at us.

"Wasn't that amazing?" he exclaimed as everyone else was settling in the van.

"Only you could come out of an eight hour 'kill me now' meeting and still be that excited, Alec." I laughed.

He shook his head and elbowed me lightly in the side.

"Aren't you tired at all?" I whispered to him.

"Nope! I am so 'effing excited. Man, this day was the absolute best. I love these meetings."

His raspy voice wrapped around me. I smiled and scooted a little closer to him. At this point, it had become second nature for us to be close. We constantly touched or looked at each other. Especially me.

I'd come to terms a while ago that I had feelings for my twenty-year-old bandmate. Honestly, when I figured it out, it didn't surprise much. I didn't have a crush on him. No, since the first day we met, we were like two peas in a pod.

One day, during a conversation with Mom, she'd suggested my feelings for him were more than friendly. I thought about it, not long, before I concluded. It made sense. He made me happy, probably the happiest I had ever been with anybody. He didn't know how I felt about him, but things were going great so why ruin it?

At this point, we shared an apartment in downtown LA. The ride back to our place took about thirty minutes, and we all slept or quietly talked about the day's events. Not long after, we pulled up outside of our apartment, jumped out, and made our way inside from the dreadful heatwave that had been going on for what seemed like weeks.

"Well, I'm toast. I'm headed to bed," Jax announced and received nods of agreement from CG and Jase as they headed off to their rooms.

"So now what, Al? Wanna watch a movie?" I asked with a smile as I walked to the living room, took off my shoes, and threw them onto the loveseat.

He nodded and went to the black shelf near the kitchen to pick out a movie. A minute later he turned to me, an evil smirk gleaming from his eyes. When he held up a scary movie, it didn't shock me. We probably wouldn't be too engrossed in the movie anyway. I settled into the couch cushions, yanking the big, fluffy blanket down from behind me.

After he put in the movie, he made his way over and snuggled beside me. I wrapped the blanket around him, leaning into him. As my head fell across his chest, his hands found their way into my long hair. A shiver of excitement burst through my stomach, so I kept my eyes on the movie. Goose bumps flew down my arms as he continued playing with my hair. He whispered my name, and I looked up into eyes so intense it made me think he'd been staring at me for a long while.

"Hmm?" My shoulders tensed as I waited for his reply.

He dropped my hair and shifted back from me. "Do you think it's weird?"

My eyebrows flew up in confusion. "Do I think what's weird?"

He motioned between us and looked away, coughing a little. "Us... you know; the way we act with each other. Do you think it's weird?"

I angled my head toward him. Why was he questioning our friendship? Why now? Since the day CG introduced us a connection snapped into place, one I'd never questioned. Even before I had realized my feelings for him, he'd been my best friend. We got along so well and had an easy, natural relationship. Since the beginning, people had given us curious glances, and when we told them we were friends and not in a relationship, the curious glances turned to weird ones. It had always made us laugh together, late into the night, as we talked about it.

"No, of course not, why would I?"

I sat up from my previous position as he looked down at me. By the way he kept tapping his fingers in his lap, I could instantly see that he was nervous. He looked down at his hands, and then he bit his lip. When he coughed again, I raised my eyes to his face.

"Well, it's just... I don't know, isn't it weird that we always cuddle and are touching each other in some way?" He looked down at the blanket as if suddenly finding the fluffiness of it intriguing, and then pretended to start picking pieces of lint off it.

I sat up a little straighter before looking at him again and responded, "Well it isn't for me; we have always been like this. Alec, why are you asking this now?"

"I don't know," he snapped, and then aggressively ran his hands through his long hair. "I have heard some things is all..." He flicked his eyes toward me, then stared at his lap again.

What? Was he afraid I would ostracize him from my life for good or something? He should know that would never happen.

"Heard what things?" I asked him, keeping my words steady and even.

"Just some stupid stuff about..." he stopped, shaking his head before looking back at the TV. "You know what, forget it." He pulled himself away from me and sat on the opposite side of the couch.

A pain encompassed my heart as I feared he didn't want to sit next to me and I frowned. "Alec, tell me."

"No, Lilith. Forget I said anything, okay?"

His glare could freeze hell's fiery depths as he snapped at me. My chin hit my chest as my vision blurred, my eyes filling with tears that threatened to spill any moment.

He noticed. "Crap... Lil... I-I'm sorry... Lil. It's just..." he paused and ran his hand over his face before looking me in the eyes. "I read some stuff online about how people think we're a couple...I mean, yeah I know we've heard some stuff before, but this is different. I mean they were calling you names...horrible names. It was—it was aggravating to read I guess."

I couldn't help but smile at how adorable he was when he was all flustered. He had a slight blush on his dark face, which never happened. My heart longed for him, but he was my best friend first and foremost, and I would never compromise our friendship like that. How could I?

"Why does it bother you so much? I mean, it's just random people, who don't know us, talking," I questioned.

"It doesn't," he responded quickly. Too quickly. His eyes widened, and he started stuttering, "I-I mean… I- We aren't… You aren't… I…"

I laughed. I couldn't stop it. His eyes widened before I pulled and squeezed him into a hug.

"I know that, Al. We know that." I smiled, playing with the back of his hair. "It doesn't matter what the rest of the world thinks. I have you and our friendship. It's the only thing that matters to me, okay? Nothing anyone says will ever change that." I squeezed his hand, and he nodded.

He went quiet for a while. I would have thought he was asleep except his hand was tracing small circles on my wrist. This usually meant he was overthinking something. I gave him time to think and let him come to me when he found a solution.

After about fifteen minutes, he sat up abruptly and met my eyes. We were close. Too close. A nervous jangle floated through my chest, but I pushed it down and smiled up at him. I tucked my hair behind my ears to keep it from falling into my eyes, and as I brought my hand back down to my lap, he grabbed it. His eyes never left mine as the smile slowly disappeared from my face. I stared at him, really watched him as his eyes never left mine, so many conflicting emotions floating through them I couldn't read them all.

"It wasn't what they said that bothered me, Lil."

He'd been quiet so long I jumped when his words wrapped around me. He laced his fingers through my hand he hadn't stopped holding.

Something about it was so much more intimate than anything I'd ever felt before. It could be wishful thinking on my part. I wanted more than friendship, but he didn't. I knew that, and it had to stay that way.

"Yeah?" I held my breath, waiting for his response.

He nodded. "It was what I felt when I read it, and what I wanted to do to those horrible people."

I tilted my head to the side as he smiled softly and scooted a little closer.

"Nothing will change our friendship, right? You mean that?" he asked.

I nodded in response, my throat so dry I could barely swallow. He inched closer and closer to me, and I could feel his hot breath on my cheek. I couldn't breathe. Didn't know if I wanted to.

"Then let me try something."

His words were soft, so soft I almost didn't hear them before he erased the remaining distance between us and pressed his lips to mine. My eyes fluttered shut.

He was kissing me. My best friend; the guy I had fallen in love with ages ago was kissing me.

That was the best moment of my life.

***

21:45

I had spent the last two hours crying and laughing while I stared at picture after picture, reliving memory after memory. Some came from the past few years with the band, but even more from before I'd met any of them.

I loved remembering each family holiday. Every laugh and prank pulled on Dad. All the best family moments came from the holidays and weekends away. Every holiday, we invited my extended family over and went to our vacation home together. Grandma would tell me I was too small and needed to eat more; my aunts would tease me about boys. My cousins would brag about getting their licenses and doing well in school. My uncles would ask if I was finally going to get into sports and join a team or two.

I couldn't imagine my parent's faces if they could see me today, which is why I hadn't visited in months. I'd also become too busy on Saturdays with album stuff and interviews, so I no longer had time for our video chats. My lips fell toward the floor as I grabbed my phone and quickly dialed my mom's number, not caring what time it was. I needed to tell them I loved them; it might be the last time.

"Hello?" a worn-out voice said after a few rings.

"Hey, Mom. Did I wake you? I'm sorry for calling so late." A shuffling sound scraped across my ear.

"Lil? Hi, Honey! Of course, you didn't. I was reading. How are you?" My mom's voice lifted, and I smiled into the phone.

She was my life-long best friend. I had always told her everything, even my feelings for Alec. When I finally did figure everything out, she wasn't surprised at all; well, she did put the thought in my head so I suppose she wouldn't have been. She only rolled her eyes and said, "It's about time you figured that out!" She always knew the right thing to say. Right now, I needed that. I needed her.

"I'm okay," the words rushed from my lips so fast I didn't know if Mom understood them.

But, she did. "What's wrong, sweetie?" She always knew, as if she had some sensor inside her when something was wrong. Mother's intuition, maybe?

"I'm just *tired*," I whispered.

"Go on. I'm listening."

As I opened my mouth to respond, a sigh escaped, but it didn't ease the tension in my shoulders. "I've been really stressed lately. I'm just sitting here looking through my photo book and thinking of you and Dad."

"Oh, honey...we both miss you to bits as well. We haven't seen you in months, and you've been avoiding our Skype calls for work and to be honest, honey, your father is starting to question why."

I flinched, my hand rubbing the back of my neck. "I know...I'm sorry. I have been distracted."

"Markus?" She spat out his name like it was a third-world disease.

I chuckled. "No, just things on my mind is all."

"Lil, you know you can tell me anything, right?"

Mom always had a way to get me to spill my guts to her, but this time I stayed quiet for a few minutes, fighting the urge to tell her everything. What should I say? What could I say that wouldn't give everything away?

I took a long, shuddering breath. "I miss *him*," my voice broke.

She sighed on the other at my response

"Mom?"

"Yes, sweetheart?"

"H-How-" I paused, unsure if I should keep going, but finally, I did. "How far would you go for Dad?"

"To the ends of the earth and back." Her response came so fast I could tell she didn't even think about it for a second. "When you love someone, Lilith, you would do almost anything for them, be anything for them."

"Would you hide it? Your love?" I asked, barely above a whisper.

"No."

That one word made everything around me shatter. Her breathing picked up.

I closed my eyes tight. "I love you, Mom. Tell Dad I love him too, okay?" Before she could respond, I hung up.

I looked down to the home screen on my iPhone. My face instantly changed into one of disgust as I saw the picture of Markus with his arm wrapped around me in Milan.

My phone vibrated, telling me I had a new text. I ignored it. I already knew what it would say, and I didn't want him to know where I was. Or else I wouldn't do this. I couldn't.

With shaky hands, I turned my phone off. Then I set it aside. I pulled out my charger and plugged in my laptop before turning it on. It took forever to load and every second that went by made my heart beat faster and faster, like it could burst through my chest at any moment. It didn't stop me from clicking on the Firefox icon and typing the address for the site I hated these days. I barely logged on anymore because I couldn't stand seeing all those people pouring out their love for Alec and me, or Markus and me, or the few people who sent me hate mail or death threats.

I signed into my account, clicked the tab for a new tweet and wrote out a super simple message before sending it out.

@OFFICIAL_LIL_ROSE: 5 MINUTES. BE HERE AND READY. XX

My mentions were quickly ambushed with questions and requests. Nevertheless, I ignored them and opened a new tab.

I typed in another web address and waited as it directed me to the site. Then I watched the clock, five minutes passing at a snail's pace, but when they did I signed in and clicked to link it to my Twitter, telling what I hoped would be most of my followers from around the world that I was online for a Livestream.

I hadn't done one of these in a long time, and I almost felt bad for the fans who would think this was a good thing. Almost. But, I needed to do this. I had to.

Adjusting my camera and turning the chat to live, I looked up to see my face on the screen and cringed. No make-up covered the dark circles under my eyes, making them stand out like a sore thumb. I ignored it the best I could.

"H-Hi, everyone," my voice came out raspy, and I couldn't focus on anything but the viewer count as it continued to grow higher and higher. Nervous energy coursed through me. I tried to shake it off and remain as calm as I could.

"I know I haven't done one of these in, like, almost six months now, and if I am going to be honest, I don't want to do one now. But I *really* need to." I bit my lower lip and lifted my eyes up toward the ceiling before eyeing the screen again. "I wanted to talk to you guys about a few things, some things that have been bothering me and maybe even share a few memories. But, before I do any of that, I need to tell you all something."

I made sure my eyes were peering directly at the camera and gave them the best smile I could muster, it never looked like it used to, but it was the best I could do now.

"I just want to sincerely thank each one of you from the bottom of my heart. Thank you for every song you downloaded, album, concert gear, and concert ticket you have bought over the years. For those of you who have been watching us since the beginning, thanks for every like and subscribe on YouTube. I don't know if I show it very often, but I am so very grateful for everything you guys do. I promise I see all your hard work and dedication. It never goes unnoticed so don't think that—ever." I bit my lip a little harder trying to hold the tears in, but they were already filling my eyes. "I love you all so very much." My voice cracked like dried paint sitting under the sun too long.

I sighed and rubbed my eyes before placing the laptop down on the bed and sitting up straighter.

"Ever since we started this crazy journey, my life has turned into this big whirlwind of non-stop craziness. Some good and some not so good. So much has happened, and it's been so hard to get used to it. I mean, going from the new kid at school, trying to find my place, and meeting this crazy awesome group of people I'm overjoyed to call not only my band but some of my closest friends. To now having cameras shoved in my face and a sea full of people chanting not only the band's name but my name is a pretty big change." A half-smile curved my lips before I continued.

"I never in a million years thought we would get this big, you know? Never thought we would have this many dedicated fans, sell this many records, or even make *four* albums. There are days when I sit down, and my mind is absolutely blown by the album charts or how many albums we have sold, and it's all due to you guys. Yeah, I mean we sing, record, and perform, but if you hadn't seen past our crazy personalities and one too many jokes to see the passion we all share to sing and perform, we wouldn't have come this far. Not in a million years. A-and to be perfectly honest, I still don't know what you guys see in us—I mean let's be honest. We're a bunch of freaks that shouldn't be able to make it in a band, but somehow, we make it work. However, I am our band's biggest critic. After living the life I have for almost five years now; it gets difficult not to critique everything I do or sing."

I let my eyes flutter down a little bit to see all the comments and questions, but I looked away. I couldn't bear to see them right now or to answer questions. I had a purpose for doing this tonight, and I was going to accomplish it.

"But I-I'm not happy anymore guys, and I haven't been for two years now." I studied anything but the camera, trying to hold myself together. "I need to tell you guys the truth. I owe you that much. We all do. I have been hiding this for a long time, and the lies I'm being forced to tell have become too much for me to handle. I-I have been forced to play the role of someone I don't want to be, someone I am not, and I-I..." My gaze fell back to the camera, tears steadily falling down my cheeks now. "I'm tired guys. I-I don't want to be tired anymore." My eyes locked on the viewing numbers and my jaw almost dropped. This was the highest number of Facebook Live, or any Livestream for that matter, viewers we'd ever had.

"You were right, all of you. And I can't stand to lie to any of you anymore so in the next—" I stopped for a moment to glance at the clock before meeting the viewer's screens again, "thirty-two minutes I want to tell all of you the truth. Every bit of it. But, that is all the time I have before I have to say goodbye."

Chapter 3

Alec

19:15

I STUMBLED INTO the doorway of my apartment, lips locked in a tango with a tall, tan redhead's. Not that I knew her name, or even bothered to ask, but I didn't need her name when she looked like she did. Man, her body was to die for.

I didn't take in my surroundings as I kicked the door shut and pushed her against the wall, not taking my lips from hers. It wasn't even eight P.M., and I was drunk, but that wasn't anything unusual. Not anymore. It had become routine.

On days like today, the pressures of my everyday life built up so much I couldn't take it. I had to find a way to forget. Taking a complete stranger to bed always did the trick. I didn't do it every night, but tonight, I needed it more than I cared to admit.

It all started with this lame ass party our label threw us for our five-year anniversary. I couldn't believe we'd been a band for five years today. Crazy. And of course, all the bigwigs were there, from our management team to the CEOs of our label. For today, they didn't mind us letting loose, so I tried to have some fun for once.

What they didn't realize was how impossible it would be for us to let loose while they were there. Absolutely, impossible.

The hairs on my neck and arms stood up while they were there. Hell, anytime they were around we were afraid they would tell us we were doing something wrong, or even threaten us. They did that a lot. And I hated it.

It was an afternoon of drinks and bull; mostly talks about the new album we were working on and what we were looking forward to on the next leg of our tour which started in August. Boring discussion after boring discussion. I couldn't escape. If I tried, I couldn't imagine the lecture that would await me the next day. But I couldn't hear any more of the same damn things, like I sat in my room with a song on repeat. So instead, I drank until the pain started to fade and their words no longer sounded so bad.

"Too close, Mr. Young."

"Watch where you're looking, Mr. Young."

"Do we really need to have that discussion again, Mr. Young?"

The words kept coming, but it didn't matter anymore because my mind spun from the drinks and I no longer cared. They could do what they wanted. Make me out to be whoever and whatever they wanted me to be. When I had so much liquid courage burning through me, none of it made a difference.

Two hours, a quickie, a slap in the face, and one slammed door later; I was finally alone. My head hadn't stopped spinning. Maybe

I'd drank too much earlier. More like I probably did, but there was a reason. I didn't want the haze to end. Not yet. And when it started to, I stumbled down to the kitchen and found a bottle of jack hiding deep in one of the cupboards. I'd known exactly where to find it since I stocked it especially for days like these. I grabbed a can of coke and mixed it with the jack in a small glass. Leaning my head against the counter, I winced as the cool liquid burned its way down my throat.

Another night alone.

I hated feeling this way: dark, alone, depressed. But lately, it seemed like they were the only emotions I could feel. I never let anyone in, never let the ones already in get out. I was cold most nights, but tonight a different feeling consumed me. Anger. It flowed through my veins, making my limbs shake. The tips of my ears were so hot I wanted to dip them in ice water.

Then came the hurt. Both anger and hurt were two emotions I never let myself feel. It's different when they've been shoved so deep down my throat I couldn't help but choke on them. Every ounce of control had been used to keep my cool today, and I still didn't know if it'd worked.

***

14:00

"Look who it is. My favorite group of *misfits*. It's so great to see you." Martin, one of our managers, approached, a fake smile plastered on his face. We reciprocated, matching his perfectly, nodding our hellos back to him.

37

"It's great to be here. Thanks again for throwing this for us." Jase's smile wasn't fake. No, he gave his award-winning, best-of-the-best grin that could make anyone light up. Except for Martin.

He waved him off with a chuckle. "Oh nonsense, you guys deserve it. Are you enjoying your break? The tour will be starting back up soon. Any new songs for the album?"

"Of course, who doesn't love some time with the fam and writing with these crazy dudes!" CG exclaimed. "I mean you're lucky I'm wearing pants! You know what they say: no touring, no gym, no pants, and all the cupcakes you want."

Martin raised an eyebrow, and a very painful grin appeared on his face when she continued.

"It's called having a balance, guys!"

I couldn't help but laugh a little at her. I had known her for most of my life, and the girl never had a dull moment.

"Right, right," he said before turning his attention to Lilith.

"So, rumor has it Markus is taking you two on an early anniversary celebration soon. Yes?"

My back stiffened at the mention of his name, but I shook it off just as quickly as it came on. I couldn't believe I'd almost let the mask slip.

Lilith, on the other hand, didn't have to hide anything. When I risked a glance at her face, a smile beamed from her; I would have said it was fake, the fakest one I'd ever seen from her, but that was back when I knew her, or thought I did. Now I could tell love and devotion glowed from her. Love that I hated. Love that I *envied*.

"Oh, right. We are going to be leaving tomorrow night for Paris," she said, her eyes shining with excitement.

"Oh! How exciting! I wish you both the best time then." Martin smirked, a twinkle in his eye. I couldn't stop the first eye roll, but after I realized it happened, I kept them to a minimum...well, as much as I could.

I shifted my eyes to see Jase staring at me with a soft look I couldn't stand, so I shook my head and found something else to study.

"Of course! I'm happy to be here in time. With our crazy tour schedule, I thought I'd have to reschedule the trip. I can't imagine what Markus would have said then. Nothing good."

A chuckle left her still smiling lips, and I clenched my fists. I sneered and groaned. And before anyone could say anything about it I turned and walked away. I couldn't stand it. I couldn't stand Lilith. And I most certainly couldn't stand her damn good-for-nothing relationship with Markus.

Time for a drink and to forget.

***

I choked down the rest of the glass and kept it in my hands, gripping it so hard I could have shattered it. Before I did, I released it, prying my fingers from the glass and setting it in the sink. My palms rested on the cool counter as my head dropped, a long sigh escaping.

When had my life changed so much? When had it become so miserable, so unbearable I barely wanted to live another minute?

I wanted to call her, or hell, I would have settled for texting her. But I couldn't. I couldn't have anything with her. I missed her more than anything. God, what I would have given for just one more chance. To go back and change it all, to say no, or to fight.

Instead of fighting, I had to forget. Forget the memories. Forget the past. Forget the present. Forget the now impossible future I'd wanted for so long. It was gone, replaced by an already mapped out future I had no choice in. One I didn't even get to help create.

Silence engulfed me, and I stood in it, let it settle around me until I couldn't stand it anymore. Turning off the lights in the kitchen, I made my way back to the living room and slumped onto the couch. The clock hadn't even hit ten. I had nothing to do, not until our flight to the UK, so I turned on the television and scrolled through all the unneeded channels until I found something I wanted to watch.

I shifted until I found a comfortable spot, watching the screen but not seeing anything. Since the show didn't catch my interest, my eyes slowly drifted closed, and I started to fall asleep until I heard a loud bang. I shot up. My eyes shifted over the entryway to see my disheveled looking moron of a brother, Jase. He lives two apartments down. What the hell is he doing here now?

"Dude! What the hell?" I yelled at him; my speech slurred slightly.

"Alec, get your laptop. Now," he yelled back at me, and I saw CG and Jax run in behind him.

"What the hell are you all doing here?" I questioned the three goons, very confused and exhausted. I should have moved to a different building across town, rather than a different apartment in

40

the same 'effing building, and not tell them where. I don't have time for them to keep coming over whenever they feel like it.

"Stop asking questions and get your freaking laptop," CG screamed, causing me to jump.

She never yelled. She never even raised her voice.

More people filed into my home and my eyes widened as I noticed people from our management team, from the label, and finally Joe, our bodyguard. They all had one thing in common. Joe may have had the calm demeanor he always carried, but his eyes told a different story. He was absolutely terrified. The others looked they were about to piss themselves.

"What in the holy hell is going on?" I asked again.

I saw Jase come back downstairs from my room holding my laptop. He plugged it in, turned it on, and navigated it to whatever had them all so damn worried.

I stood there more confused than ever, looking at anyone, everyone, for answers. Until he stepped back and I saw the last thing I had ever wanted to see in my life: a crying Lilith on the screen. My eyes widened further as I took in her appearance. Messy hair. No make-up. Dark eyes. A tear-stained face. Trembling lips and hands. And my shirt. *When did she take my shirt?*

"I-I have been forced to play the role of someone I don't want to be, someone I am not, and I-I," she stumbled off.

My heart shattered into a million different pieces as more tears fell down her face. What was she doing? Why was she crying? I moved toward the screen, not taking my eyes from her.

"I'm tired guys, I-I don't want to be tired anymore." She looked at the camera, showing the world her eyes, once so beautiful, so bright, but now...now they were so dull hardly any life shone out of them.

"Lil," I whispered even though no one was paying attention. What was she tired of? Who could make her feel this way?

"You were right. All of you. And I can't stand to lie to any of you anymore so in the next—" she stopped for a second to look down at something before looking back, and I could have sworn she was looking straight at me, "thirty-two minutes I want to tell all of you the truth. Every bit of it. But, that is all the time I have before I have to say goodbye."

A slow tear trickled down her cheek, and my knees gave out. I dropped in front of the laptop, staring at her beautiful face. I didn't know what she could be saying. Thinking. Feeling. But I couldn't take my eyes off her, not even for a single moment. My heart stilled. I froze, scared even to breathe.

I waited for her next words even though I didn't know if I wanted to hear them.

"...before I have to say *goodbye*."

An invisible knife plunged into my heart, taking every bit of hope with it.

Chapter 4

Alec

Three years ago

SUNDAY HAD ALWAYS been my favorite day. No worries threatened to crush me, and with nothing to do, I could relax the day away. Ever since I was a little kid, I lived for Sundays and the tradition it brought. No matter where my family and I were or what we were doing, we'd meet up in the living room for Sunday dinner, a movie, or a family game.

As time went on and Jase and I got older, it was sometimes the only time Mom and Dad could get us all together. But, when the band finally took off, everything changed. We hadn't been able to go home on Sundays. At first, it tore me apart. I missed family day so much, which made everything with the band difficult. But three amazing friends stepped up to the plate and helped fill the empty hole in my heart even when I didn't need it filled anymore. I had Jase too, like that one fly buzzing around my head over and over no matter how many times I swatted at it. I chuckled as I reminded myself to tell him about the fly thing.

One Sunday, I got so down I sat on the couch and didn't move for hours with my head rested on my hand. I never even turned the TV on. No, I sat there in utter silence staring at nothing, so lost in my head I couldn't find a way out. I missed my family. I missed "our Sunday", and I couldn't handle any of the band stuff anymore. I even thought about quitting.

But I kept it all in, never telling anyone. Not even Jase. I figured they'd make fun of me. I mean, I couldn't argue. Even I knew I was acting like a girl. Sometimes, emotions ran deep, sucking you into a bottomless void with no hope of getting back out again.

Another Sunday, as I swam in my pool of despair and watched a movie, CG became my lifeline.

I wanted to be alone, but as she plopped down next to me, we both knew I wouldn't turn her away. And she was relentless, pestering me to tell her what was wrong. One thing I had learned about Chloe-Grace was when she wanted something or wanted to know something; she would damn well get it out of you, one way, or another.

I spilled my guts that day, my emotions so raw by the end my eyes blurred, and my bottom lip quivered. Somehow, I held the tears back. When the rest of the band came in, I let out a relieved sigh. I couldn't imagine what they'd think if they saw me crying, but I hadn't known they'd heard the whole conversation.

Everyone sat around the room, telling stories about how hard things were on the road, especially being away from their families. I remember the shocking jolt that pulsed through me when Jase admitted he felt the same way as I did, missing movie days and Mom and Dad. I wasn't as alone as I'd thought, and I didn't need to seclude myself.

The real bonding happened that day. More than anything else, we became closer, and for me, I realized having someone to talk to might make things a little easier.

Jase and Jax picked out a movie, popped it in, and we sat together, watching it. Nothing could ever replace family Sundays with Mom and Dad, but making a new tradition helped ease the pain from missing home.

Today we were all supposed to hang out, the same as every other Sunday, but everyone had other plans. They all cancelled, well, except Lilith and Jaxson, but the latter wouldn't leave his bedroom. When the doorbell rang, I answered it to find a pizza delivery boy. I had to pay and carry it into Jaxson's room. I guessed he needed his "lazy Sunday" this week.

Lil never failed me though. She made us both some homemade spaghetti and put my favorite movie in. I smiled and slid into the couch, grabbing her favorite blanket from the back. I could never be upset about some alone time with my favorite person in the whole world. I sat on pulled her against me. A permanent smile settled on my lips every moment I was around her, but since the day I'd told her how I felt, the smile never faded, only grew bigger and more radiant.

***

"Alec? What's got you off to Wonderland?"

I jumped, so lost in my thoughts, Lil's voice startled me. I turned to her. "Hmmm?"

"I have been trying to get your attention for a couple of minutes now. I thought you were mad at me for something and I couldn't figure out what it could be. You had this 'I'm Mr. Serious' look on your face. Had me all kinds of worried."

The drawn eyebrows made her forehead scrunch and her eyes do some weird stuff. I couldn't help it, I burst out laughing.

Her bottom lip jutted out as she crossed her arms over her chest. Snaking my arms out, I turned her to fully face me and pushed myself on top of her, hovering a good ten inches over her. A shy smile sparked on her face, but she shrugged with indifference even though I could hear her heart thudding.

I angled my head so my lips rested against her ear. "Actually, I was thinking about you." I paused to watch the blush spread from her cheeks to the rest of her face. My grin grew as I continued. "How amazing you are."

The red hue of her cheeks darkened to crimson. This happened every time I complimented her, and I loved being able to have that effect on her.

"Not this again. Will you st— oh no! It's so embarrassing," she groaned, swatting me in the chest.

I laughed so hard I couldn't catch my breath, but when I did, I pressed a kiss to her forehead.

"Your reaction is worth it," I smiled and rested my forehead against hers, her breath fanning my face when she started laughing.

"Will you ever stop teasing me about that?"

I shook my head in response. I couldn't look away from her.

Instead, I stared so hard into her eyes I could see the love, so much love, reflecting back at me. How did I never see it before?

"You know what I don't want to stop teasing you about, like ever?" she whispered to me in a teasing tone after a few minutes.

"Oh, this should be good. Tell me, Rudolph, what will you not stop teasing me about?"

She stuck her tongue out at me like we were back in the fifth grade.

"I never want to forget your reaction when you realized you kissed me. I have never seen you blush or stutter so much—not in all the time we've known each other."

A smirk threatened to stretch over her lips, lips I couldn't take my eyes off of, but somehow, she held it back, wrapping her arms around my neck.

"So, how about a redo? Seriously, I'm down any day of the week. I mean, of course, I would need my camera to show your brother and the others because no one would ever believe that Mr. Bad-to-the-Bones can actually be nervous or embarrassed."

"Oh no. Don't you know? That never really happened. It was all in your head." I pressed my lips together to hold back my grin.

"Oh really, now?"

"Really." Still fighting the smile threatening to give away my hoax.

"Well I know the truth, and I will never let you forget it, even if I have a camera ready at all times now."

I gazed at her a moment, letting her see the half-smile I lost the battle with. Then I crashed my lips into hers, trying to erase that dreadful moment from her mind, even though I didn't think she'd ever forget it.

Chapter 5

Alec

22:40

MY EYES WERE wide, my hands shaking. Whispers and gasps surrounded me, but I didn't pay attention to them. All I could see, all I could even think about, was Lilith, sitting behind her laptop in front of me. Her lifeless eyes stared into the camera right in front of me. Maybe she knew I'd be watching. Maybe she hoped I would. Either way, my eyes never left hers. They didn't even falter. I stared straight at the unmoving screen, unable to look away even if I wanted to, which I didn't.

Shouting broke out behind me from people who cared about her and from some that didn't. They wanted to know what her plans were, what was happening right now. Well, so did I. Maybe they should watch the screen.

Our managers were trying to find her but no luck so far. Their yelling wrapped around me and at one point I thought I heard my name but nothing registered. Not one thing. Except for her mouth, opening and closing in front of me like she wanted to talk. I didn't want to miss it if she did. I wouldn't. So, I drowned them out until their chattering became too much.

"Will *you* shut the fuck up?" I snapped, my frozen body finally breaking free.

My heavy breaths weighted my body, releasing a guttural sound from me I'd never heard before. Tears streamed down my cheeks like drizzle before a storm. My heartbeat sped up so fast it reminded me of the seconds of a timer ticking down until a buzzer went off. My buzzer might make my heart give out, though.

My thoughts had encompassed me so much I hadn't realized the commotion and yelling had come to a crashing halt. Everyone faced me, waiting for me to explain my outburst, but I didn't have time for it. I wouldn't take my eyes off the screen and Lilith, afraid I would miss something if I did. Nothing else mattered to me. Nothing. Her words had become my lifeline, and if I didn't hear them, I'd fade. These lowlifes and their big mouths wouldn't make me miss it. I wouldn't let them.

"I guess now I am at the point of telling you everything, but I really don't know what to say or where to start." She took her eyes away from the camera. "So, I guess I will start from the beginning of this crazy journey, yeah?" She leaned against a headboard.

It was the first time I allowed myself to look at anything but her. I studied her surroundings. She wasn't at her apartment.

"When I first met the guys, not too long after CG introduced us, it was a bit awkward, as most of you might expect. They all dressed like they came straight out of Hot Topic or a punk rock magazine, and I looked like I came out of Hollister. If any of you saw us together, you'd have laughed. I laughed. However, they were in a band. Well trying to be. They just needed a lead singer." A smile made her eyes glow. I hadn't seen her smile like that in a long time. "I'd always loved to sing. I never went for it because I thought my vocals were too weak. After they booked their first official gig and they still lacked a lead singer, CG suddenly remembered hearing me sing a bit earlier in choir, so she told the others I was alright and convinced them to give me a shot. I was terrified. I mean, there was no way I could live up to their standards, right? They had a certain image, played a certain type of music. But I—I suddenly knew—I needed it, to be a part of something and I was beyond excited." She paused for a moment, her face lighting up.

"I knew when they voted me in as lead singer my life would change. I didn't care about any of that, though. I was gaining four new, crazy, awesome friends. I couldn't have been happier."

She shifted on the bed, resting one hand on her knee and the other on the bridge of her nose. She looked so fragile, but a glimmer shined from her eyes as she talked about us. I felt someone brush against my arm as they slid to the floor next to me, and as I glanced over, I saw crazy, wild, electric blue hair; I knew it was CG. Her brother, Jaxson, sat next to her and Jase on the other side of me, everyone eyeballed the laptop.

"With that decision made, we went to our first cover gig to make it official. We did a cover of a Green Day song together; one you guys probably already know. I mean, it is our *favorite* song to cover,

'Boulevard of Broken Dreams'. It sounded so cool, mainly because we sounded good together. We decided it was time for us to celebrate. Guess what we did?"

I felt a smile tug at my lips as the one on her face grew a little more. She let out a hearty laugh while looking off camera. "Before anyone says anything... no, we did *not* go and get matching tattoos. We went and got pizza and sat in the restaurant almost all night, talking, and just had a great time."

Focused on every move she made, I didn't miss the frown tilting the corners of her lips as she gazed into her screen.

"I realized then how close we would be. I knew, no matter what happened with United Misfits, we would always be friends. We would always be in each other's lives. Especially one of them in particular."

She bit her lip and met my eyes through the camera. At least, it seemed that way.

"Alec..."

As she said my name, I tensed.

"He and I just—you know, we just connected. Well, to be honest, I'm not sure that's the right word. Maybe *gravitated* toward each other. It was almost magnetic for me. Like something pulled me to him. I didn't know why or even what, but I couldn't help it. I wanted to be around him all the time. He always made me smile and laugh like I never had before. He was such a funny guy." She smiled into her memories.

"We sat by each other all evening that night. While all of us were talking and they were welcoming me into their secret group. It was like we already had our own inside jokes. Like we had known each other our whole lives, and we knew each other's secrets. It was an instant friendship."

Murmurs broke out behind me again, so I turned and took it all in. Everyone whispered together, some with annoyed looks and some with wide, fear-filled eyes. Were they scared of what she might say next? With a shrug and a shake of my head, I twisted around, facing the screen again.

"Pretty much everything after that was caught on camera. Whether it was on our YouTube channel, or after, when our luck changed, and we signed with Star Records and Management six months later. Our friendship grew and melded together. We had so much chemistry, it was like nothing I had ever seen before. We supported each other throughout the whole process. We needed each other for the hard times following our big move. Being so far away from our families wasn't easy. No amount of solo fame would buy out the second family I had gained. They became my life. To the end, no matter what, I will stand by that." She smiled into the camera.

"Has anyone tried to call her?" Jaxson asked from my right.

My brother nodded. "We did," he motioned between himself and CG. "Her phone is turned off."

I sighed and looked back at her face on the small screen.

"After we got signed and the big move to LA, everything got so intense. You know?" she said. "We continued to make covers for our YouTube channel, but we started working on our own album, writing our own songs, doing fan meet and greets, having crazy long meetings, and add a media tour to that—we were overwhelmed and super busy right off the bat. Although we loved it, it was a massive change we had to go through. But we embraced it fully. But, after a while, some things changed in our little group." She stopped for a second, looking like she was debating something in her head and suddenly bit her lip. "The rest of the band started to change."

I sat back against the couch on the floor in confusion. What in the holy hell was she talking about?

"I started noticing some weird things going on around the house. Whispered conversations in secluded hallways. I couldn't help myself, one day I tried to listen in on one of them and was extremely shocked to hear what I did." She paused for a moment, running her hands over her face and softly laughed. "Man, they are going to kill me when they find out I said anything. Between two of my bandmates, I started seeing something happening."

My eyes widened, and next to me, CG stiffened. I risked a glance toward her. Her face had turned so pale she resembled a ghost in the middle of a haunting.

"No, no Lil, don't do this. *Please*," CG whispered.

When I looked back at the screen, Lilith's next words made my jaw drop to the floor. "One day, I accidentally walked in on Jase and Chloe-Grace kissing."

Holy–

"Shit."

I heard my brother finish my thought aloud. The murmured

conversations going on behind me grew louder and louder, spilling into the room in a cluttered mess of mingled words. I couldn't hear Lil anymore, so I turned the laptop's volume to max, or would have if it hadn't already been all the way up.

"I couldn't believe what I had witnessed, and believe me; they still don't know that I saw." She let out a soft laugh. "However, the thing is, I wasn't upset that they hid it. As weird as it sounds, I was quite relieved. I had been coming to terms with my own feelings, which had been swirling inside me for quite some time. The two of them only sparked the flame inside me even more. They gave me the confidence and the extra boost I needed to accept what I was feeling." Lilith suddenly stopped speaking and looked around the room, as if contemplating what she wanted to say next.

"Is it true?" My eyes jerked from the screen to land on my brother then to CG, but they didn't stay on her long as I met my brother's gaze once more, and then over to Jaxson. Jaxson's eyes grew as he looked at the two of them in disbelief. They nodded their heads wearily in confirmation.

"How long?" Jax asked with a harsh tone.

I could hear the anger and betrayal laced through his words.

Jase gulped as his chin fell to the floor, which had become his main focal point.

"Since... since the night we got signed," the words came out a whisper, almost like an exhale, but I heard them loud and clear.

"What?" Someone behind us roared, and I peered over my shoulder just in time to find Martin storming through the door.

Everyone in the room froze. Except me, I couldn't freeze with anger making my limbs shake. I couldn't even look at the guy without my jaw clenching.

"Since the night you signed on?" his yelling turned into a solid growl. "You damn well better be *joking.*"

CG and Jase both shook their heads, but their eyes remained on the floor.

"How could you not tell us? Especially *you,* Jase. I expected more from you."

"Oh, fuck you, man. Like I would tell any of you twisted racist people. Honestly, the only thing you seem to be worried about is making your next big buck!"

Jase surprised me by yelling even louder than Martin. I mean this wasn't expected, but why the hell is he so angry? I didn't have to be facing him to tell how angry he was, and I didn't have to be his twin to figure out what was going through his head either. But, before anyone could say anything else, Lilith's voice made the room fall quiet.

"They helped me realize I was in love and I should be more confident about it. But it scared me. I didn't want to admit the truth to anyone. So, even though I accepted the feelings I had, I kept them hidden." A smile flashed across her face. "Inside, I screamed it. I was in love with my best friend, with Alec. But only I could know it at that moment."

A small smile tugged at my lips. Those six words always made me grin, but I hadn't heard them in so long. The storm raging inside me dissipated when she said them, but I had a feeling it would only be a matter of time before the winds picked up once again, sending my soul straight into oblivion.

Chapter 6

Alec

22:35

I NEVER THOUGHT words alone had the power to both heal and destroy me all at once. They always said actions spoke louder than words, and in a certain light I believed that to be true. To me right now, her words had become the catalyst to make my heart beat again, but they also held the power to destroy my very soul. Never had anyone physically harmed me, I'd never let that happen. But today, it had only taken simple words to punch me in the face so hard I crumbled to the floor.

Now, unable to draw breath, I realized all it had taken was Lil saying my name and love in the same sentence. I'd been desperate to hear it, but at the same time, I never wanted to hear it again. Did that make any sense? To me, it did.

Love's destruction had pulled a number on me. It had made me weak and so vulnerable. It had always made me feel the same. It still did—vulnerable.

"This is ridiculous," someone mumbled behind me. "Someone needs to find her before she throws her entire career out the door."

Those words made my spine stiffen. Everyone beside me looked just as rigid, like starched clothes after they'd been ironed.

"Her career? *This band*? Is that really the only thing you can think about right now?" Jaxson suddenly spoke up from beside me. "*Something* is bothering her, hurting her. She's upset and unstable, obviously, and all you idiots can think about is her career. Who the hell cares about her *career* right now? I bet she doesn't." He paused, breathing so heavy he couldn't speak. When he gained control, he continued. "Our best friend is God knows where telling the whole world everything about all of us. *None* of us know why. But, I would bet all the money in *my* bank account that it has nothing to do with *her career*."

The momentary happiness flew right out of me. I hadn't wanted to think about it, but Jaxson was right. Something had to be wrong with Lilith to make her do this. I just had no idea what it could be. Nobody did. I also didn't know what she planned to do here by telling everyone our secrets. I had a bad feeling swimming through the pit of my stomach. I'd been trying to shake it, but I hadn't been able to, ever since I first laid eyes on this live video.

"How about instead of standing here worrying about your next dollar, you do your actual job and 'effing find her," CG snapped, pulling me from the thoughts that threatened to drown me.

As I placed my hand on Jaxson's arm, he looked at me. Something on my face relaxed his features, and the tension fell from his shoulders. He pressed his lips together and frowned before we both glanced back at the screen.

"I guess once I accepted it, it was obvious that I always fancied Alec. I mean, what wasn't there to like, right?" A low chuckle fell from her mouth as she beamed at the camera. "He made me laugh all the time and somehow, he had this built-in sensor that told him when something was bothering me. He knew how to lift my spirits, and he made it so hard to be upset when I was near him." She shook her head, grinning from ear to ear now. "And it wasn't just me. He brought out a bubbly giddiness in everyone around him. Nobody stopped smiling from the moment he entered a room. I did keep it a secret, though. I was afraid if I told anyone, especially Alec, they would laugh in my face. I'm not sure why since they are the most accepting people I know, but it frightened me." She bit her lip, pausing for a moment before she continued.

"But, then one evening while Alec and I were watching a movie, he kissed me." She laughed. "I remember feeling shocked and almost frozen with it. I couldn't believe it happened. After I'd dreamed about it so long. And let me tell you, the dreams did nothing to prepare me for the real thing, which was a million times better than anything I thought up in my head." She winked, and a rosy hue spread across her cheeks. I inched forward, as close as I could get to the screen.

"Some people might find it weird. I mean, we were bandmates and best friends, but I swear the moment our lips touched—the world shifted. Everything we'd lost had fallen back into place. Never had I felt the amount of love and passion and warmth..." she shied away from the screen before meeting it head-on again. "Nothing could compare to it. It became a memory I cherished and held onto above all else. One I'll never forget as long as I live. Of course, it is one of my favorite ones of Alec and me."

"I can't believe she is telling everyone this- Holy fu-, guys look at the number of people watching. There are well over two million now," Jase interrupted, his eyes locking with mine. "Alec, you need to do something." He narrowed his eyes. "This could end badly, Alec. People, as in *you*, could get hurt."

I stared openly at him, my mouth half opened and my eyes unfocused. "What am I supposed to do? Her phone is turned off. She's only paying attention to the Livestream."

"Maybe type in a comment? See if she sees it?" CG shrugged. "It's worth a shot."

I bit the inside of my cheek for a few seconds but gave in, leaning forward as my fingers glided along the keyboard.

LIL, PLEASE CALL ME. -ALEC

It was all I could think to type. Her eyes scanned the screen, but if she'd seen it, she didn't react. I typed the same thing again. Nothing. Either she saw it and ignored it, or she had so many comments coming in mine was lost in the sea of letters.

"So, um...after our kiss, you would think things would be a bit awkward, right?" She smiled. "Never with Al and me. Like I said,

61

everything just fell into place. We never had a long conversation about what we did. We never asked what we were. We were together after that. Simple and easy, like everything else with Al. Neither of us even asked the other out. We were just a couple. And let me tell you, I was over the moon." She twisted strands of her hair around her fingers, still grinning.

I smiled right along with her, knowing how true her words were. We clicked into place like Legos, building our relationship with each block, and it worked. For a while.

"We kept it a secret from everyone because it was new and we were still figuring it out. We didn't have a clue how anyone would react. Plus, our first album was set to release later in the year. Everything snowballed around us. We didn't want to add to that, even though we knew we'd have to tell everyone soon enough. It was funny when we did tell because, all CG, Jase, and Jaxson did was just kind of stare at us like they thought we were going to say something else. I think CG's exact words were, 'You made me almost piss myself for something I already knew.' I don't think I've ever laughed harder or been more relieved. Seems Alec and I weren't as clever as we thought, and everyone already knew something was happening."

"Everything went on as normal, except we kept our relationship between us, the band, and our families. We weren't ready for the world to know yet, and definitely not ready for our management team to know. So, we played it off as a friend-lovefest type of thing. I don't even know what to call it. People questioned it, but we just told them we were best friends. I think everyone believed it for a while, but the comments started pouring in. You guys became infatuated with the idea of Alec and me. You wanted it to happen, which we found amusing since it had been happening, but it also scared me. Us. Know what I mean?" She paused for a quick second before she continued. "We were afraid that we would lose fans because of all the hate floating around the internet. We couldn't let it ruin our career, the band's career. All of us wanted to be successful, and we wouldn't be if this continued. So, we didn't spill the secret, but it was getting harder and harder to keep. It even put a strain on our relationship, and I hated it. I hated knowing it hurt Alec because we couldn't hold hands in public, or we couldn't go on a date because people would speculate. Everything we did felt wrong because we knew what would happen because of it."

She sighed again as she gazed around the dimly lit room.

"So that's when we decided we needed to come clean with our management team. We had to tell them we were together and in love because we needed it out in the open. It was hurting not only our relationship but our friendship. I mean, even the others could tell the strain the secret had put on us. They encouraged us to tell them, but we were absolutely terrified. It's hard enough to come to terms with it all yourself, let alone wait for the approval of others."

I leaned forward. I wanted to hear this even though I knew what came next. I'd sat in the room, after all. But, I also knew Lil better than anyone in the world. She was hiding something... Something that even I didn't know.

Lil cleared her throat, drawing my attention back to the screen. "So, when the end of fall came, we set up a meeting with our management team. We sat down with them to talk about our career, which shifted to our personal lives. After, Alec and I came together, spilling everything about our relationship. We told them we were in love and happy all while wearing the sappiest grins on our faces and stealing glances at each other. We told them we wanted to be honest with them and with our fans. We wanted to let the world know we were a couple."

With a flick of her head, she stared into her lap. "In that meeting, they plastered smiles on their faces and told us congratulations. In that meeting they said they were happy for us, it would all be okay. We just needed to decide how to tell the public." A look of pain flashed across her face.

I scrunched my forehead, barely able to breathe. What had happened? I could tell by her words something had happened after the meeting, but I had no idea what it could be.

A hitched breath drew my attention to Jase, but the minute I met his eyes, he closed his, looking toward the floor. What was going on?

I angled my head. "Jase?" my voice cracked.

With tears in his eyes, he peeked at me, shaking his head over and over. "I'm sorry Alec."

I pulled back, my eyebrows pinching together on my forehead, but didn't press him. I gawked at the screen instead.

"After that, Alec and I left hand in hand, smiling so big our jaws hurt from it. I was so happy, a never-ending peace washed over me. Until the next morning."

I stiffened.

"The next morning, I got a call to come back to the office. Management needed to see me. I thought it was strange, but I shrugged it off, thinking it was probably nothing." Her bottom lip trembled. I wish I had never gone back into the office...I wish I wouldn't have sat down and listened to the bull story they gave me. But I did."

"What is she talking about?" my frantic voice pierced the apartment as I gaped around the room, not sure who to look at first. "She told me she went to get breakfast, and she came back with donuts. She couldn't have gone to a meeting." Silence answered my questions.

"When I sat down in the chair across from Martin, Alice, and a few others, I thought maybe they needed to go over a few things about our relationship. To an extent, I was right. They did.... They told me it couldn't happen. They said they wouldn't let it happen. Alec and I couldn't be together, not then, not now, and not ever."

The air whooshed from my chest like someone just punched me. My mind moved in so many directions I couldn't pick one. Nothing added up. How could any of this have happened and I didn't know about it? How? I didn't know, but I kept quiet, listening even more intently.

"They told me they worked out a plan to change the way I felt about Alec. I just laughed at them and their ridiculous notion. How can you make someone change the way they feel? We were in love! You can't just change that, and I knew they couldn't make me feel any less in love with Alec than I did. But, they said they were going to try." She swallowed hard but met the camera head-on with focused eyes.

"They handed me a thick stack of papers—*another contract*. A stupid contract that I had to sign, and if I didn't sign they said they would pull me from the band. They said I could easily be replaced. Girls would line up for the chance. I shook my head at them. I didn't believe they could replace me. They couldn't take me from the band, could they? Well, my fear got the best of me when they showed me things. Things fans had written about me. Hateful things. How I didn't belong in the band. My vocals were weak. I was fat. I didn't fit in. I never thought it would influence me, but at that moment, it did. What's worse is Martin, Alice—every one of them—knew it would. They'd put their heads together after Alec and I left the night before to find my weakness, to figure out how to break me, and they succeeded. They did what they had to do to get me to sign the contract and I...I did. I signed it..." her voice cracked.

I don't know when I moved, but I stood in front of Martin, staring hard at him. My breaths came fast and hard, looking past him and around the room at everyone standing there with sheepish looks.

"What did the contract say?" I demanded, my fists clenching and unclenching at my sides. "What. Did. It. Say?"

Not a single one of them would meet my eyes, but every one of them had pressed their lips together.

"What did that damn contract say?" I yelled past my dry throat.

I waited for an answer. Any answer. But not a single one of them gave me one. Instead, the only sound came from the sobs from a broken girl on a Livestream who felt the need to tell the world her story. A girl I thought loved me, but instead had left me. A girl I gave everything for and had broken my heart into tiny pieces when I thought she'd left me on her own. A girl who left me with nothing to live for.

None of them gave me an answer, but she did. "The contract said I had to end everything with Alec, our relationship, our friendship, everything. I had to be with someone else, another boy—a *white* boy—who was better suited for my image. For the *band's* image. Someone who wouldn't cause controversy. I had to make Alec believe I'd never loved him, that I was too good for him. That I'd forgotten him."

My vision swam in front of me, anger fueling it. I launched across the room toward the man I now hated with every part of my soul. I didn't look back.

Chapter 7

Alec

MY HANDS HOVERED inches away from Martin's neck. I couldn't stop thinking if I did it, if I choked him out, it would end my misery. I wanted him gone. The world would be better without him. I couldn't think about the repercussions of what I was about to do. The only thought floating through my mind was to hurt him. Just like he hurt me. But mainly for hurting *her.*

"You good-for-nothing little piece of—" I flew back as someone pulled my shirt, yanking me into a solid body. I struggled, but couldn't break free. I'm kind of glad I couldn't because right then and there, I would have killed him. Nothing would have stopped me. He'd ruined my life, Lil's life, and who knew how many more on top of it.

I gasped for breath, finally gaining a little control. "How could you?" my voice shook.

"Alec, I think it's best you calm down."

Martin's calm tone made me scoff. I sneered at him.

"Calm down? You really think after what I just heard I can calm down?" The only sound in the room came from my breathing. My face heated so much it felt like I could fry an egg on it, even the tips of my ears were hot. "You forced a contract on her? *You* broke us up?" I tried to wiggle free, but strong hands palmed my shoulders and arms wrapped around my waist. Probably for the best. I didn't trust myself at this moment.

Martin shrugged as if he didn't have a care in the world and a sinister smile formed on his lips. "It was for your own good and the good of the company,"

"The company? Our relationship had nothing to do with the company. We were happy. In love. And you ripped it all away," I growled and all but stomped my feet.

"Oh, come on! You didn't possibly think we could let the two of you be in a relationship. First, you're in a band together, so one wrong move or argument and *bam,* the band's done. Second, give me a break. You couldn't have believed we could let two of the most talked about members of United Misfits become a powerhouse couple. For God's sake, you're *black* and she's *white!* It would have ended in a disaster. No one would have supported you. We may have come this far, but no one is ready for that. Look at the way the world is, son. The riots and police officers. The last thing we needed was your fans to go crazy because you're too ignorant to see that you need to be with someone of your own kind," he spat the words "black" and "kind" out as if it were some disease.

I yanked free from the people, my friends, holding me and launched forward, almost falling face first. Only then did I see Joe step in the middle, blocking me from Martin and staring at me with hooded eyes.

"Alec, you know this won't solve anything," Joe whispered. "Just take a few deep breaths and let's focus on the most important thing right now, okay? Finding Lilith."

The anger pumping through my veins simmered to a slow burn. At that moment, when the room quieted, the sound of Lilith's sniffles brought me back to myself.

I gave a curt nod to Joe before turning around and seeing the others behind me with wide eyes and tear-stained faces. Not hurt by me but hurt for me. We always tended to feel what the others in the group felt. That was just how we worked together, how we helped each other out. Although, maybe I needed to work on my role since I'd believed Lilith's lie for so long.

Lilith. My amazing, sweet, loving Lilith.

The others stepped aside, and I looked back to the laptop, seeing her with her hands over her face. Shaking my head, I looked back at Martin and every piece of filth standing around him. All of them played a part in this. Every last one of them.

"You really think this is for our own good?" I croaked, pointing a shaky finger to Lilith. "Did you think so little of us—of me—that you had to do this, because of the color of my skin? You pathetic piece of—"

"Alec."

It had come from Lilith's sweet voice. I rushed back to the computer, dropping to my knees in front of the screen.

"I loved him so much, you know," she said in a tiny, almost inaudible voice.

A gaping hole erupted from my chest. She used past tense. *Loved*.

"We were so happy, and everything was perfect. I never stopped smiling or just generally being happy while I was with him, but that day, everything came crashing down. I felt like my life had stopped while everything and everyone around me just kept moving, but I stood alone. I had to break my boyfriend's heart and in turn, break my own."

A whimper escaped even though I tried to hold it back. The tale she was about to tell—I didn't want to hear. I already had to live through it once. I kept those memories hidden deep inside, but it looked like I might just have to relive the most horrible day of my life. Again.

***

Two years ago

Lilith had been acting strange the past few weeks, and I couldn't figure out why. Whenever I asked her, she put on a forced, fake smile or she told me I was over analyzing things, over analyzing my ass. I knew Lilith better than I knew myself. Something was wrong.

So, I decided tonight I'd get some answers. I would make dinner for her and give us a night to ourselves. We hadn't been alone for a while. I missed it, so maybe she did too.

I spent all day shopping and cleaning up the apartment. Then I told everyone to stay out to ensure we were alone. I didn't want any interruptions. It might be cheesy, but I even lit some candles and made a bed of pillows and blankets in the middle of the living room floor.

Everything turned out perfect. Even the spaghetti and meatballs tasted delicious. I put on some nice clothes, new jeans with a button up white shirt and made sure my shirt had no wrinkles. Tonight would be special. I'd make sure of it.

I winked at the mirror. "Someone is getting lucky tonight." I rolled my eyes. "Yeah, not if I keep saying stupid shit like that."

I did a little shake to make the nerves fly off me. I couldn't figure out why I was so nervous. I had never been before. Butterflies, sure, but they were different.

All the questions vanished from my mind when the jangling of keys and clicking of the lock on the door sounded through the apartment. I rushed out of my room and waited in the middle of the living room. When she stepped inside, I couldn't stop the gangly grin from spreading across my face. Her eyes widened as she took everything in, from the pillows on the floor to the table steaming with hot food, to the lit candles. Her mouth parted slightly as her hand came up to rest on her chest.

Then her eyes met mine. "Al... Are those candles? A-and rose petals?" she took a deep, trembling breath.

I glanced at my feet, biting my lip. "It's too girly, isn't it? I knew it. I should have gone with pizza and a movie." I bent over the table, about to blow out the candles, my heart dropping as I realized she didn't like

72

it. "Don't worry. If we call now, they should be able to get it to us in about half an hour, and you can pick out a movie on Netflix. While you do that, I-I'll just throw all this out," I mumbled, unable to meet her eyes.

"No," she jogged in front me, grabbing my hands and pulling them to her.

She kept my hands against her but glanced around at everything I'd done again. A smile broke out on her face, not the fake one she'd been sporting the past couple of weeks, but a real one that made her eyes glitter. When she gazed into my eyes, I thought I might shatter.

"It looks beautiful, babe." She placed a soft kiss on my cheek before pulling back, not taking her eyes from me.

"You like it?" my voice still held the nerves I couldn't shake. Maybe she just said she liked it so my feelings didn't get hurt.

"No. I don't like it. I love it. Everything is amazing. Babe, did you do all this for me?" she angled her head.

I nodded. "I just thought maybe we could spend the evening together? Just us, like we used to." I stepped closer, wrapping my arms around her waist.

A light blush shimmied across her cheeks. "But only if there is food. I swear I could eat an entire cow right now," she chuckled.

I laughed hard. Maybe a little too hard. "Do you know me at all?" I led her to the dining room table, showing her the spread. She sat down and dug in, so I followed suit.

We ate our dinner together with more heartfelt conversation than we'd had in weeks. We laughed and talked well into the evening, and soon it passed and turned to night. After we finished eating, we moved to the living room hand in hand. We kicked off our shoes and laid down next to each other on the pillow-covered floor. I flipped to my side, staring at her, taking in every line on her face. She looked at me the same way, studying everything about me, memorizing it.

"I've missed you the past few weeks. We haven't really been together a lot," I whispered, my heart trying to beat out of my chest. "I just like spending time with you, Lil..."

Lil frowned. "I know, Al. I've missed you too. I-I just think everything has finally gotten to me, you know?" She looked anywhere but at me.

I reached forward and pulled her close. Her head nestled into my chest. We didn't move for a long time and instead laid there, afraid to let each other go. I could feel something shifting. I just wasn't sure what.

Occasionally, I leaned down, placing a gentle kiss on her head and running my fingers through her long blonde hair. I adored this girl. She was everything I could've ever asked for in a girlfriend: funny, kind-hearted, and real. I never knew I could feel this happy, that such happiness existed. But with Lil beside me, it would never go away. Soon, we could share that happiness with the world. Then all the stress would disappear, along with the secrets.

"Lil?" I shifted, nudging my elbow into the ground and leaning my head into it.

"Yeah?" she pulled back, her brows raised.

"I love you," I paused, waiting for her usual immediate response. But, it never came, even after several silent seconds passed.

I nudged her playfully. "I said I love you," I frowned as I felt her pull away. I sat up, crossing my legs and staring at her still lying on her side. "Lil? What's going on?"

She stayed quiet, twirling a blanket around her fingers. "Alec. I..." she stumbled over her words. That was when I saw it. Something passed over her face, and when she finally met my eyes, my heart dropped so fast it took my breath away.

"Alec, I met someone else."

I flinched. "You w-what?" I couldn't have heard her right.

"I said I met someone else; do I need to spell it out for you?"

Each word she spoke was like a punch to the gut. I could barely breathe, barely move. When I collected myself, anger surged through me like a bird trying to escape winter. "You're lying. You and I are—we're together—a-aren't we?" My heart hammered in my chest.

"Look, Alec. This was fun while it lasted, but that's all it was—fun." She shrugged like it was nothing. Like we were talking about politics or the weather or something equally mundane.

I jumped to my feet, staring at her but not able to see her. This couldn't be my Lil. No way.

"Lil, what are you talking about?" Somehow, I kept my voice calm, my tone even. It didn't last as more words screamed through the room, from my own mouth. "We've been together for a long time now. You can't be serious. I love you. You love me."

"You honestly thought I loved you?" she laughed. "You're even more pathetic than I thought." She shook her head while pulling her black boots back on.

A cold dread coated my stomach. "W-what are you saying?"

"Oh my God, Alec! Do I have to spell it out for you? I. Never. Loved. You." She rolled her eyes. "How you thought I actually did is beyond me."

I stumbled over to the table and leaned against it, needing something to keep me upright. I couldn't feel anything. My legs. My heart. Everything was numb. This couldn't be real. She couldn't mean anything she'd said. Could she?

I shook my head vigorously, as if I could shake this whole nightmare away. Then I stopped. I just stopped and looked at her with blurry eyes. "But you told me you did."

"I lied. Ever heard of it? It's easy to do, especially when the receiving party is so naive." Her eyes roamed from my head to my toes, and she smirked, her eyes were so mean I didn't recognize them as hers.

I squeezed my eyes shut, surrounding myself in darkness. A tear slipped down my cheek, but I refused to let any more follow. I couldn't let her see me fall apart, and I was seconds away from an utter breakdown.

When I opened my eyes, Lil bit her lip, her eyes sad, but it lasted only a minute before the cold look passed over her face again. I rubbed the back of my neck.

"Sorry if I hurt you or whatever." She flicked her head. "I mean it was fun and stuff, but I found someone else, someone I want to be in a real relationship with. You know, long-term."

I didn't know what to say or do. I couldn't move, not even to collapse into a heap on the floor. She only stood there for a second more before she grabbed her jacket and slung it over her shoulder. With one last glance my way, she made her way to the door.

I snapped out of it, rushing forward and grabbed her by the arm, not hard, but enough to stop her. "You know as much as I do that we are real." I gestured between us. "This is real."

She jerked from my hold and reached for the door handle. She shot a look of true hatred at me, her tone as she spoke so deathly cold, it could freeze a graveyard. "No Alec. We aren't. We never were, and we never will be. I don't love you, and I never have. Trust me. You're not my type. The person I love will have bigger dreams and actual goals he wants to accomplish. You aren't capable of that."

She spun, storming from the apartment. The door almost hit me in the face.

***

Present Day

The pain in my chest felt just like it did that day, but this time, I couldn't stop the tears from falling. I'd tried *so* hard to block it out, to mask my emotions and bury them so deep inside myself I could never find them. I'd done well for a while, but hearing the story from her fragile voice—it brought it all back as if I were there again, in that room. She remembered everything. So, did I.

Jaxson sat beside me, his arms wrapped around me. I couldn't look at him, I could only stare at Lilith, crying even harder than I was.

"I didn't mean it, not one word. Nothing I said that night was the truth" her voice cracked and sputtered, like a car with a bad starter. "How could it be?"

I didn't think I had ever cried this much. My head dropped into my hands, the warm tears dripping between my fingers.

"Alec, I don't know if you're watching, and I honestly pray you aren't, but if you are…"

I raised my head slowly, meeting her eyes.

"I swear I didn't. I know it doesn't make sense right now. But I promise, it will."

Chapter 8

Alec

I SAT THERE frozen, just staring at the screen, every second, every minute of that day playing on repeat in my head. Each word, each painful strike left my heart filled with holes, ones that never healed and were hidden. And now, hearing it all again, felt like a sharp piece of glass had slashed every wound back open again.

I'd believed every single word she'd spat at me that night. I'd believed she didn't love me...that she never had. And I took her word when she'd told me I meant nothing to her, thinking it had all been some sick game she'd played with my head. But it hadn't been. And now, now I couldn't feel anything.

"I knew exactly what I had to say and do to get Alec to believe me. I still can't believe he did, though. How could he believe I never loved him?" her tone deepened with a hint of anger. "Had I not shown him how much he meant to me? How could he believe my lie so easily?"

I closed my eyes, bowing my head. I rubbed the back of my neck, unable to come to terms with the fact I had believed her lie. But she'd told it so well it had been hard not to.

"When I walked out the door that night, I knew I'd destroyed him. You have no idea how hard it was. How much I wanted to turn back and run into his arms. To kiss him and tell him it had all been a lie. To explain I'd never, ever say such hurtful things to him on my own..." she paused, running a hand through her hair, "But I could do none of those things. Because if I did, I'd never be able to see him again. And it seemed better, even if I couldn't have the relationship I wanted with him, to at least keep our friendship. To not lose him from my life forever." She shook her head. "That's when Markus came into the picture."

I jerked up, every bit of flexibility leaving my body. As stiff as I was, I don't know how I glared at the people behind me, but I did.

I hated Markus. He'd been the reason she'd left. The other guy. Well, I'd thought he'd been, guess I'd been wrong. So, wrong. And now I felt like just another fan watching this. I had no idea what she'd say next. Already, her story had been very different from the one playing in my head. I didn't know anything anymore.

"Markus... he is a nice guy and all, but—to be honest, he isn't what I wanted. He had never been *who* I wanted." With a flick of her head, she glanced at the screen with focused eyes. "Once again, you, the fans, had seen right through everything. Every date was a publicity set up and all the tweets, pictures, everything was done by *Star Management*." She gave a half-smile. "I don't want anyone to hate on him. He has become a good friend, honestly. Since day one, he's known how much I loved Alec and been there to talk to me about all of it."

80

A movement caught the corner of my eye. I peered behind me and saw Markus moving through the room. Tears flooded his eyes but didn't spill over. He held his phone in his hand, and I knew he'd been watching, just like we all had been. He took his eyes from the phone and stared at me. My chest felt heavy, and I didn't have any words. Not yet. Lilith's voice pulled me back to the screen.

"So many nights when we were supposed to go out, we spent in his apartment, sometimes mine, with me crying and him holding me, talking me through my tears. Some nights I couldn't do anything else. But somehow, through his words, I started to believe there might be a day when everything would be okay. That one day, Alec and I would be together again." A chuckle fell from her mouth. "You'd be surprised how big of a fan he was of ours." She glanced back down.

I eyeballed Markus again. As I continued to stare, I couldn't stop my face from contorting until a harsh glare hit him head-on. Markus looked at his feet, unable to meet my eyes. I couldn't blame him. I probably couldn't have held my gaze right now either. But, the anger coursing through me, pumping my heart into a staccato beat that wouldn't be held down.

"Get out," I seethed.

"A-Alec, if you'll just let me—" he started.

I stopped his words with my own. "No. I don't even want you within twenty feet of me, much less in my apartment. I'll say it one more time. Get. The hell. Out." It took everything in me to stop, to not scream at him. I hated him. Lilith's story would never change any of that.

He nodded and stared up at me with a helpless look as his arms went limp at his sides, but it did nothing for me. Nothing. I am not the others. That pathetic look won't work on me.

"I just want you to know the only reason I agreed to the whole thing was because I thought you would have felt better knowing I was with her, someone who cares for her instead of someone who would treat her like crap," he said.

I let out a loud laugh and stood, facing him.

"Really, Mark? Can I call you Mark? Well, Mark, that would be funny, because if I remember correctly, when we first met, you told me 'she was a nice piece of ass' right before you found out she was my girlfriend, so don't think I'll play into your pathetic lies like everyone else." I took a few steps, but stopped, digging my heels into the ground to keep from moving any closer.

"Oh, don't be so petty, Alec. That has nothing to do with this," he pointed at the screen.

"Oh, really now? Like you wouldn't have jumped at the opportunity to be with her all while making a *few extra bucks*?" I held up my hand when his mouth opened to respond. "Don't. I don't want to hear it. Your mind games might have worked on Lil, but they'll never work on me."

"I came here to help, not to be yelled at."

I rolled my eyes. "You want to help? Take your bull and get out of my house. Maybe jump off a bridge. Better yet, don't come back and never, ever contact any of us again. That would be great, okay?" I turned away, dismissing him.

He might have left. He might have stayed. I didn't pay attention, but instead, I watched Lilith again, clearing my mind enough to try to figure out what was going on with her. Really going on. There had to be a bigger picture in all this.

"Even though the pain still swam through me, Markus and I began to go out, to date. To let everyone see our faces. And then our album released. We had our first worldwide tour coming. I plastered a smile on my face, at least as much as I could, but every time I looked at Alec, it faltered. You know he was never great at masking his emotions."

The sound of her laughter caused a smile to stretch across my face.

"The one thing I knew how to do, and do well, was hide my feelings and emotions. From everyone. I was a master of telling lies and could sell a story to anyone in the world, be it the media, the band or you...the fans. It was never as easy as it seemed though. Especially with Jase."

When Lilith paused, I furrowed my brow toward Jase, but my brother wouldn't look anywhere near me.

Lilith cleared her throat, drawing my attention again, and she took a long swig from a bottle of water. "You see, Jase knew everything. Management needed someone to keep an eye on Alec and me, to make sure I was upholding the contract I signed. Who better than Alec's brother?" She pressed her lips together. "I was glad in a way. It gave me someone to talk to other than Markus, but it also made hiding my feelings much harder." As she finished, I felt my jaw clench as I looked over at my brother. I saw CG and Jaxson staring at him, equally wide-eyed, but nowhere near the level of anger I was about to reach.

My jaw clenched when she stopped talking and I stared Jase, my family, my blood. "You knew? This whole time? And you never said anything?" The words tumbled from my mouth in a scream that echoed through the room.

He finally stopped watching the floor and met my eyes, his chin quivering. "I'm sorry, Alec...it—it wasn't my place to tell."

"Not your place? You're my fucking brother. Or did you forget that little detail? We are supposed to tell each other everything. Not keep secrets! Or maybe that's a one-way thing." I could probably have pounded a hole through my wall, and I could hear my heartbeat through my ears. Not good. I needed control.

"Look Al, I'm sorry! At the time, I thought I was doing the right thing!" He wiped at his nose. "And if you did find out, if I did tell you—there was no telling what you'd do. I-I was afraid it would tear the band apart and..." he cast his eyes to the ground and pressed his lips together, not able to finish.

It took me a minute to stop the shaking in my arms. I had to breathe deep. Inhale. Exhale. After the minute passed, I wasn't shaking anymore. I knew the real reason he'd kept the secret. "You thought it would tear you apart from CG."

He nodded, biting his trembling lip. I wanted to stay mad at him. It would make things so much easier to have an outlet for this rage soaring through me, but I couldn't. I understood the feeling of not wanting to be apart from the one you love. More than anyone.

"But, eventually, I mastered hiding things from Jase, too. Maybe if I weren't so good at it, things would have turned out different. I doubt it, but there's always that chance, right?" Lilith scratched the side of her face. "See, that day in the conference room with Martin and the other members of Management, I stared at that contract for a long time. I weighed my options, but I didn't have many. Not with the things they had to persuade me into signing. It hurt. Way deeper than I ever thought something could hurt. Caring what people think about me has never been my thing. I'm unique, and I like it. Always have. Always will. But those words that day...they cut deep and stayed deep."

My ears perked at the muffled conversations behind me, and I turned to see Joe speaking with a few policemen.

"We've checked her credit cards and everything; she hasn't used them which most likely means she used cash. Look, she obviously doesn't want to be found," the police officer said.

"What about her car? Any sign of that?" Joe questioned, and the officers shook their head. Joe gave me a soft smile before turning back and lowering his voice.

"I've promised I would be honest tonight, and I want to be." Lilith chewed on her bottom lip. "I just don't want you all to hate me for sharing this stuff. It's so personal, and no one knows about it. Not Alec, Jase, or any of the boys. Not Markus, and definitely not my family. I'm the only one..." she closed her eyes and pinched the bridge of her nose with her fingers.

"The night I left Alec thinking I didn't love him, I was broken. I couldn't think, move, or even breathe. My chest felt like it had caved in. Everything became a struggle. I just had to take one simple breath. But I couldn't. And I didn't think I'd ever be able to again. I mean, I was breathing, but it felt like an elephant had sat on my chest." She took a long, shuddering breath. "I drove around town, stopped a few places before landing at a stupid five-star hotel. I did some things that night, some things I wish I hadn't," she shook her head and rubbed her forehead. "I-I'm not the strong person everyone thinks I am. It's all pretend, and the person I pretend to be isn't me. Never has been, never will be. I'm sorry. But, every emotion in the world shifted through me when I got to my room and wouldn't stop. I hated, and still hate, myself for what I did to Alec. I wanted to be punished for it, to suffer for making him feel the way he did."

My sweaty hands clenched into fists as I watched her with wide eyes.

"I needed to feel the pain Alec felt, and I needed to feel mine." She let out a bitter chuckle. "Honestly, I don't remember much of what happened after I got to the hotel. I woke up the next morning with a throbbing headache and blood-stained clothes to match my new scars." She rubbed the back of her neck. "I never thought *I* was the type of person who would self-harm, you know? To be honest, I always thought people who said they needed to self-harm to feel pain were ridiculous, but that night—I understood. I felt pain inside, but it was my own. What would make *me* feel better." She clenched her eyes closed, releasing a few tears. "It didn't make me feel better," her voice splintered. "Every day I woke up, my heart reminded me what I did. I had to see Alec every day, and I could see how sad he was. Another reminder for me. But, I also had scars on my body now too, reminding me even more who I'd become and what I did."

"No," I whispered. "No, no, *no.*" I gasped for breath, pulling at the collar of my shirt. There was no air in this room. I couldn't breathe.

"I continued with it, hoping it would start erasing the pain. Day after day, but always over the same cuts, so nobody noticed. I hardly ate, and I stopped interacting with fans. Then I withdrew from everyone. Being alone, with no one around me, helped me to not spread my misery. And it was the only time I could be myself." She closed her eyes again. "I just couldn't bear to see the hurt in Alec's eyes and the confused and angered looks of Jaxson and Chloe. I stopped living as much as I could without actually ending my life."

I sucked in a breath and placed my hand over my heart.

"I'm sorry," she said, sadly looking down. "I'm sorry I lied. The day I ended things with Alec, everything from that point on has been one big lie. I've been the biggest lie of all." She bit her lip as she sat back, adjusting the computer on her lap.

My eyes caught on a piece of artwork on the wall behind her. It looked familiar. I tilted my head to the side, trying to place it.

"I've done things in my life I'm not proud of, but hurting Alec—it was the worst thing I've ever done. I love Alec more than anything in this world. Never stopped. He's the best thing that ever happened to me." She met the screen with big, sad eyes. "I'm only sorry I didn't fight harder for you, Alec."

Silence fell over the room. I held my breath, waiting for her next words. They never came.

"Oh no! Alec." CG's frantic voice pulled my attention to her wide eyes, staring at the screen. "Look at the time on the Livestream."

Chapter 9

Alec

TIME STOOD STILL. I never believed anyone that said it, but I found out the truth of it as Lilith went quiet. Everyone around me ran through the room, a frenzy of activity and movement I could hear, but it didn't make me do anything but stare at the screen. People left the room. People talked to each other in whispered conversation. I couldn't stop staring at the damn screen. Time might be standing still, but the clock still ticked with each passing second, like a never-ending wave in an ocean. I couldn't break the sheet of ice freezing me in place.

I wanted to scream. I wished screaming would stop the clock, but I knew it never would. A clock can't hear my screams. Probably Mother Nature's way of saying *screw* you.

When I finally turned, I realized I now sat alone. My eyes shifted back to the screen, making me feel a million miles away from reality. And, somehow, I felt like I'd lost everything all over again. It couldn't be possible, could it?

The cards I'd been dealt were pretty crappy, but I still played them as they came. I didn't turn and run the other way or throw the cards on the table, demanding a re-deal. I might be weak, but for the people around me, I tried to be as strong as I could. Otherwise, they might crumble right alongside me, and I couldn't let that happen.

I had already lost everything once in my life. I wouldn't do it again. Not this time. I will fight harder than I'd ever fought before. This time I'd win.

My hands were moving faster than my brain as I pulled out my cell phone. I tapped an app I knew all too well, one all our fans spent most of their time on. My nimble fingers shook as I typed out a tweet, hoping it would reach my followers.

'HELP ME. SEND A MESSAGE IN THE COMMENTS AND TELL HER TO CALL ME.'- ALEC

Short and to the point. Only a few seconds passed before my screen exploded with notifications. Twitter flooded with so many responses coming in I thought my phone might freeze, and that didn't even count all the tweets of love and devotion coming from so many strangers. But they were determined to help, even though they'd never met me.

A lump rose to the back of my throat, and my eyes stung. I set my phone down, peering back at the screen. Lilith was still sitting there but didn't say anything, only played with her shirt. My shirt. "Come on, Lil..."

"It's almost time for me to go." Her soft voice sent a shiver down my spine. "But before I do, I'd like to show you something. I hope it will be a beautiful reminder to all of you." She turned her head, grinning through her tear-stained cheeks. "Some of you might even find it romantic."

Footsteps pulled my gaze back to reality as I saw CG tread across the room to the TV and turn it to the news. Lil was on the news. The *actual* news, making headlines with her story. I didn't care, so I turned back around and watched Lilith once again.

"I wanted you all to know the true story, so you'd know what really happened and why I acted the way I did. I think I succeeded or, at least, I hope I did. Maybe I finally did one thing right," she shrugged, furrowing her brows before shaking her head. "No, that's not right. The only thing I've ever done right was loving Alec."

My breath caught in my throat as more tears threatened to spill over in a sob. Emotions plowed through my body, so many all at once that I didn't know which one to focus on first. I'd never felt any of this before, but I knew I'd never forget it.

"Yeah, that's right," she gave a feeble nod. "The thing I wanted to show you, I guess, is my last salute to this whole situation. Everything has finally caught up with me, and it's all too much. I can't take it anymore. My mind has shut down, and I feel the rest of my body shutting down with it. I don't enjoy life anymore. Honestly, I don't remember the last time I have." She clenched her eyes shut.

"I know some of you won't understand because, from your eyes, it looks like I have it all, doesn't it? I know. I get it. I have an incredibly loving family whom I miss, and will miss, dearly. I have beautiful friendships I cherish so deeply in my heart. We have fans all around the world who devote so much to us, but, even with all that, I don't have the one thing that I want—Alec." She groaned, wiping furiously at her eyes. "I keep getting sidetracked. So—"

My eyes dragged from one corner of the screen to the next, taking in everything. She stood, tilting the screen to make sure she showed on the camera.

A nagging feeling hit the back of my mind as I focused on the picture hanging on the wall behind her again. There was something about the room. "Hold on...I know that room..." Shuffling sounds rang out as people piled back into the room.

"What do you mean, Alec?" Joe asked from beside me. "You've seen it before?"

"I've *been there* before." My brain clawed through memories, but I couldn't grasp any of them enough to make them solid.

It was the painting. I knew it. I knew it when I saw it before. I knew the walls, the color of them striking a chord within me. Even the chair Lil stood in front of looked more than familiar, but I couldn't put my finger on where I'd seen these things before. I growled in frustration, wanting, no, *needing* to remember. But I couldn't.

"So back to what I wanted to show you. For those of you who've stuck by this whole '*Lilac*' thing, I'm hoping you'll understand what it means. I had to talk myself into doing this, maybe even more than I had to talk myself into doing this Livestream. But I needed to do it. I needed to prove you can't take something as big as love away from someone just because you may not agree with it." She bit her lip and gripped the bottom of her shirt. "I got this so maybe you'd understand, so maybe Alec would." She took a deep breath, and her voice hitched as sobs crashed through her body. "I'm sorry it has to come to this. I never wanted it to. I never meant for it to end this way. I'm sure most of you watching just wanted a good show. *I'm sorry-* I'm so *so* sorry," her face scrunched and then her shoulders squared. She lifted my shirt from her body, removing it just enough to show her small stomach.

I could see her ribs. I'd never been able to do that before. My forehead scrunched with my confusion, not sure when this had happened to her. The air rushed from my chest as my eyes widened more than I thought possible. More gasps rang through the room, like a gun shooting off all its rounds.

My eyes scanned her, staring at her disheveled hair and following to her dim eyes and red, swollen cheeks down further to the middle of her stomach where one word had been carved into her skeletal-thin stomach.

A tattoo. Just one word yet it spoke volumes. Everyone standing in the room with me knew what it meant, and I felt its weight pull me down with it. One word.

Courage.

Her hand skimmed across it, and she looked at the screen once more. The last of her spark, the spark that had made her seem so alive, drained from her body. It was gone, almost as if it had never existed before.

"Joe..." I croaked. "I think she's going to..." I couldn't finish the sentence, but his loud footsteps told me he'd moved forward. When

93

his hand touched my shoulder, he squeezed, giving me a little of his strength. Strength I needed at this moment.

"Alec, you *need* to remember where that room is," he spoke firmly.

I did need to remember, but I couldn't. A sheet I couldn't pull off had been laid across those memories.

"Courage," Lilith said, a sad smile touching her lips. "I have to find my own right now, but I'm also admitting I'm the biggest coward there is." She stepped forward, kneeling so only her chest and face showed. Her eyes scanned what I assumed was the comment box.

My fingers snaked out, typing message after message for her to call me. My messages flashed by in a sea of a thousand other messages, pleading with her, but her eyes widened, and her mouth dropped open. She'd seen my message. She must have, which meant she knew I was watching.

"Please, Lilith. Just one call. Please," I said aloud, begging her even though she couldn't hear me.

One call was all I needed, but as she shook her head, I knew it was a call I wouldn't get. Not today. Maybe not ever if I didn't remember where that damn room was.

"Loving you was the best decision of my life. The time I spent with you was the happiest I've ever been. Nobody could ever imagine how great it made me feel to be with you." She stared straight at the screen, speaking to me. Each word dove straight to my heart, tugging on every string.

"But this is my final goodbye..." she said so softly I had to lean in to hear her. "I love you so much."

My heart accelerated in my chest so much if it had wings it would fly away.

"I'm sorry guys."

The screen went black.

Chapter 10

Lilith

IT WAS DONE. I set the truth free like I'd wanted and now entered the final stage. I had waited so long to let the words tumble out of my mouth. An invisible weight had lifted off my chest, and I could breathe normally for the first time in forever. I'd been scared to tell the truth, but now that I had, my chest rose and fell freely. No restrictions, no rules, nothing but freedom. Every rule, every guideline I'd been made to follow over the last few years had stretched around me like a vine, choking me into submission. The more lies I told, the stronger the vines grew. The more I hurt, the harder they were to break. And instead of loosening, they grew tighter and tighter until I couldn't pull air into my lungs anymore.

When I'd finished my story, the vines had snapped. They'd never choke me out again. Everything from the past four years rolled off me in waves. A new sensation came over me, and I couldn't stop the smile from stretching across my lips. And this one was real, the first genuine smile I'd had in so long. I liked it. I hated to hurt, but it seemed all I did recently.

I knew this feeling of bliss would be short-lived, but I closed my eyes and basked in it anyways. My mind cleared instantly, letting me sink into nothing but comfort and peace. I'd craved peace for so long, but even now it didn't entirely belong to me. But it would, as soon as I finished what I'd started with the Livestream.

When my eyes opened, I took in the closed laptop, the journal, and the photo album sprawled across the bed. It all hit me. I couldn't believe I'd just told the world the whole story. Nothing but the truth and all that. What have I done? I knew they'd want more of an explanation, but I didn't have any more in me. I already poured my heart into a stupid Facebook Live Chat in front of the whole world, and the band. They'd been watching; I saw the messages, but I couldn't respond. I couldn't give him any more hope. Not when I didn't have any left to give. Hope was a fantasy, a make-believe world where I didn't live, and it was even farther gone than I was.

Standing up, I collected the last few items I had, placing them neatly together on top of the bed. I wanted the band to have them. I wanted Alec to read the journal and see the pictures. I knew they'd find me. I wasn't dumb enough to think they wouldn't. It was only a matter of time now. Leaving these things, the only personal items I had left, would give them something to hold onto when they were hit with the hurt that would follow. They'd be able to see the love in these mementos and know my choice had been my own. Hopefully.

The weight of this dark night sunk back into my chest and filled me with pain. I wrapped my arms around my stomach. It wasn't only emotional anymore. No, it had become physical. I tried not to think about it too much, but I couldn't help it.

My thoughts turned to my mom, my friends, and Alec. I always thought of Alec. His beautiful face would always stay with me, and his sweet smile would lighten every dark day to come. It might be selfish, but I hoped his heart would be mine forever. No might be about it; I knew it was selfish. But I couldn't help feeling it anyway.

At the same time, I hoped he would move past this. I prayed he didn't blame himself, but I imagined he would. He had always been so hard on himself, thinking he caused everyone's problems. And then he'd always try to find ways to fix everything. That was just who he was. He was a selfless person who wanted the best for everyone he'd ever met, no matter how briefly.

I hated seeing the way the media, and even some fans, portrayed him. He'd never been a heart-breaker, he'd never been searching for his next catch, and he wasn't a sex addict. But he was made out to be, especially after our break-up when he'd had a different girl on his arm every night. It wasn't true. None of them knew the Alec I did. The one who stayed up writing song lyrics until four in the morning. The one who went to hospitals to spend time with sick children, or the man who gave money to the homeless on the street. No, they never recognized any of that. But that was who he was and the reason I adored him so much.

I wished I didn't have to leave him, to break his heart even more, but I had to. I couldn't stop this madness if I stayed. I made up my mind a long time ago. I was finished with this life. I'd lived the perfect amount of time, even if the last few years were mostly in pain. I was done. I had no fight in me anymore. I could let go now with a free conscience. I didn't want to stay here for another miserable day. I wouldn't be a puppet for Martin, and the rest of Star Management, anymore. Most importantly, I wouldn't walk through another day shouldering all the pain, all the trouble I bring everyone I come into contact with. My fans. My bandmates. My friends. My family. Markus. The pain would never be worth the trouble I'd become.

This was the only way to end the suffering. Alec's pain would dissolve without me in the world to bring him more. He wouldn't have to sit on the sidelines, watching me with someone else, even if I'd been faking my happiness. No, I couldn't do that to him anymore, so this was our solution. The only solution. This was our way to patch things up. Everyone would go on and eventually be okay. I knew Alec would linger, but even he would find the strength to carry on. He'd done it before, and he could do it again. I knew it. I felt at peace with my choice, and I wasn't changing it.

With my mind settled, I grabbed my bag and made my way to the small bathroom. This bag had been packed for months, filled with choices since I couldn't make a decision. How does one simply decide how to end their life? It was hard enough to make the decision that my life needed to end, but to choose the method seemed out of my reach back then. Locking the door behind me, I placed the bag up on the counter and looked at my reflection in the mirror. Staring back at me was less than half of the girl I used to be. My face was drained of life, and my eyes were lost. No happiness or humor filtered through me anymore. There was no trace of the girl who used to be able to feel something other than misery. All that remained was a sad, pathetic person who didn't deserve anything she was ever handed.

I thought I worked hard for what we had, but maybe they just dragged me along for the ride. Maybe I was just there. Drifting along as I listened to the words they said about me:

Ugly

Fat

Pathetic

Useless

Talentless

Horrible

Annoying

That was what they thought of me. I was nothing but a burden on anything I touched. Even now, as I walked deeper into the tunnel, I still felt like a burden. A storm brewed from what I just aired. I shook my head. They wouldn't have to worry about it much longer. It would *all* be over soon.

I told myself it was for the best as I opened the bag. A chill rolled down my spine as I pulled out the items I'd inside, setting them on the counter. A sad chuckle escaped my lips as I thought about what would come next. I never thought I'd be doing this. Contemplating suicide. Was that me? How could that be the best solution? Why did it seem like suicide would solve all my problems? Because I wouldn't be here. That was why. I wouldn't be here. I wouldn't have to hurt or cause pain. I wouldn't have to see the pain of what I'd done showcased every day on my face. No, it would all be done, gone, dead.

I'll be dead.

I knew it was what I wanted and now, I glanced over at the clock on the wall, 23:24. I turned my attention back to the items on the counter: a full bottle of pills, razor blades, and a rope; now all I had to do was choose which way would be the quickest and easiest. And which way I wanted to end everything.

Chapter 11

Alec

I HAD NEVER been more terrified in my life than I was at that moment. All the experiences I'd been through, like posting videos and praying people subscribed to our channel, performing at local restaurants or bars, even talent shows (one talent show in particular where we caught our big break). The first one people hadn't booed us off the stage. Even going through all of these things, none of them prepared me for this moment. I couldn't speed it up or slow it down. I just had to live it, to find the semblance of hope buried deep inside of me that might give me the outcome I wanted. My gut feared I'd find the worst when we got to Lilith's room, though.

My mind raced with visions of what I would see when I walked inside, which scared me far worse than anything else. My heart pounded in my chest. I tried to place my hand over it to drown out the sound, but they were so heavy and shaking so badly I didn't dare move them. So, I sat there staring out the window of the car, hardly blinking, so empty inside I couldn't even describe the feeling.

When had I started depending on a single person even more than I depended on myself? It made no sense. I'd thought myself to be strong, a person who could take care of himself, but maybe I'd been looking through fogged-up glasses. I most certainly didn't live for me. No, I existed for her. She'd become my purpose in life, my only purpose.

We raced by car after car, police sirens blasting my eardrums. I peered out the front window, taking in an ambulance weaving through four lanes of traffic. My stomach lurched, so I looked away to make it stop, but it didn't. I was nauseous, and not because of the zig-zagging ambulance. Worry hit me hard in the stomach, but guilt tore at my soul until I couldn't think of anything else. This happened because of *me.*

What else would possess her to do something like this but me? She claimed she was doing it because she loved me, but how could anyone want to end their life because they loved someone? Nothing made any sense. If a person loved someone, they'd do anything to stay with them as long as they could. You don't take yourself out of the equation and expect it to make everything better.

Hot anger rose from my toes to my forehead with no place to escape, so it just swirled through me. Over and over. My cheeks were so hot, I wished I could stick my head out the window. How could she be so selfish? Did she not understand how much I loved her? How much I lived, breathed, ate, and dreamed for her? How the band needed her? Maybe none of that was enough. Maybe *we* weren't enough...

Tires screeched, and my seat belt dug into my chest, breaking my thoughts up. We'd stopped in front of the hotel. My mouth went dry. At least a dozen police cars parked in the lot along with two ambulances. People filed out, scattering like mice looking for cheese. I turned in a circle, spotting something in the distance. The car we would use to sneak away.

"Joe, that's her second car," I shouted.

I unbuckled my seatbelt and threw it off me, hearing it clank against the window before I pushed the door open and bolted out. I hurried toward the entrance but jerked back as someone grabbed my arm.

"Let go!" I spun around, glaring at Martin with every bit of hatred I could muster. I yanked my arm from his grasp.

"Stay out of the way and let us deal with this," he spoke as if we were in another one of our meetings.

"Let you deal with it?" I inched closer, so my face was right in his. "Oh, what, you mean like how you dealt with it last time and caused this hell hole?" I snarled as I grabbed a fist full of his shirt.

"We have no idea what she's done. You might not want to see it," he continued, his voice oddly calm.

"Listen, I don't care what I walk in on. But I need to be there. *If* she's alive, she needs to know I'm here for her." I ran a hand through my hair.

Joe sidled up to me, and together we watched a group of officers make their way inside. I turned back to Martin, my eyes narrowing to slits.

"You've already kept us apart for too long. I won't let you do it again." I sidestepped around Martin and rushed toward the main entrance.

Joe kept in step beside me, and I knew he agreed with me. We ran up to the front desk where a policeman stood questioning the receptionist. My labored breathing made it difficult to pull in air, and the room spun in front of me. I stopped for a moment, staring hard at the receptionist. She met my gaze with wide eyes.

"I-I'm sorry, sir, but that's confidential," her shaky voice came out loud, but not confident.

I gritted my teeth, biting my tongue to stop myself from screaming at her. Who cares if something is confidential when someone's life is on the line?

"I understand, but this is an investigation, miss," he said calmly.

"Unless you have a search order, I can't release customer information." She folded her arms across her chest and glared at all of us.

"Dammit," I growled. "Just tell us already!"

She jumped, her wide eyes turning fearful, but I didn't care. I would have laid into her some more, but a gentle hand on my arm stopped me. Joe. I scowled at her and waited, but still, she said nothing. I didn't have time for this crap, so I turned and ran through the lobby to the staircase. People shouted my name from behind me, but I ignored them.

When we'd been forced to work out, I hated it, but today made me thankful for it. I barreled up the stairs to the third floor, taking two steps at a time. Muffled sounds trailed me, but it didn't deter me or slow me down. Instead, it made me go even faster. I prayed I would get to the door, and she would open it, smiling and take me in her arms, planting a kiss so fierce against my lips it would make up for everything that had happened the past three years. And if that didn't happen, I prayed this had all been an awful nightmare, and I'd wake up right when the door opened. I didn't think either of my hopes would come to pass, though.

I halted in front of Room 327. I had no idea if this was her room, but it was the only thing I could come up with. *This was the only thing that makes sense.* I could see a light shining from the bottom of the door as my fists repeatedly pounded against it.

"Lilith!" I screamed at the top of my lungs. "Open the door."

I kept banging my fists on the door loudly. Other doors in the hallway opened, people stepping into the corridor with confused or irritated looks, but I couldn't pay attention to that. I could only face forward, lashing out at a door that in my way of getting to Lilith. She had to be in there. I just knew it.

"Open the door!" The tears dripped from my cheeks, soaking into my shirt.

I kicked at the door, banging the bottoms of my feet against the cheap wood as I slammed my shoulder into the center of it. But still, no response came.

"Help me!" I bellowed through my tears over my shoulder.

Joe came over and worked with me to break down the door. Side by side, we slammed our shoulders into it until it buckled beneath us. I fell into the room, crawling to my feet. My eyes scanned everything, but I knew as I saw on the laptop lying on the bed that I was in the right place. My breath hitched as I plowed forward, not finding her anywhere in the room. I searched all around, and as I turned back to look at Joe, my eyes widened.

His head tilted toward the floor, and he held one foot in the air. One soaked foot. I examined the floor below him and gasped. He stood in a stream of water with more and more coming out with each passing second, stretching under my own feet. I angled my head and could hear the distinct sound of running water. Placing a hand over my rapidly beating heart, I inched closer and closer to the bathroom door and turned the handle slowly, but it was locked and wouldn't budge.

"Lilith!" I yelled louder than I ever had before in my life. "*No, no, no!*" I repeated over and over as I beat against the next barrier blocking my way. One more to go. If I could only get through—I didn't know what would happen when I got through. Had I even made it in time? Was I too late?

This door was harder to demolish than the first, but I wouldn't stop until it was out of my way. Joe was next to me in an instant, lending me his strength. Water slushed out through the bottom of the door and the color looked a little off.

"Fuck." More kicks, bangs, screams came from me as we pounded the door down.

My body vibrated and hummed, so much adrenaline pumping through me I didn't think I'd ever slow down. I couldn't lose her, even thinking it ripped my heart apart. Dealing with the loss of her as a girlfriend had been bad enough, but at least I could still see her. But this…if I lost her like this…I'd never recover. In fact, I'd probably be right beside her as soon as the door opened, finding a way to end my own life and join her side.

Sobs wracked my body as we gave one final push, causing us both to stumble into the bathroom.

"Holy mother—" Joe whispered.

My eyes snapped to where he was looking. "No!" I groaned. Then I dove forward.

An open bottle of pills laid on the floor by the tub, and inside, drowning in milky-red water, laid my one true love. I moved faster than my mind could keep up. My hands trembled, my vision blurred and a haze-like a fog had trickled into the room. A sour taste hit the back of my throat as I gently lifted her out of the tub, and Joe turned the water off. I laid her on the floor atop a baby blue rug, smacking her cheek lightly to wake her up. She didn't respond, didn't even move, so I leaned down, listening to her chest, but I couldn't hear any breath sounds.

"Lilith! Wake up." I shook her shoulders, willing those beautiful eyes to open. I repeated the words over and over, sobs making it hard for even me to understand what I said. Tears dribbled onto her pale, white face, and I lost track of them as they mingled with her already wet face.

I was still begging her to come back to me when people flanked us, ripping her from my arms. I reached forward, trying to pull her back to me, but I was pinned back. I could see they only wanted to help her, but my insides quivered at the thought of anyone besides me holding of her. She belonged in my arms. Now, forever, always.

"*No!* L-Lil," I sobbed, trying to reach out to her. "P-Please," I whimpered as my final attempt.

My sobs didn't quiet as I watched them strap Lilith onto a gurney and began to work on her, trying to stop the bleeding. The older man told the younger he didn't know if they'd be able to keep her alive long enough to make it to the hospital. I wondered, not for the first time, if I'd made it in time.

Chapter 12

Alec

HOSPITALS. THEY GAVE me the shivers. They were a place of the unknown, of a fate one can never change. The brilliant white walls waited to be splattered with blood. The waxed floors were far too shiny to be normal. And the people who walked the halls looked either fake or miserable. Then there were the waiting rooms, the families slinking in lounge chairs while nurses and doctors bustled about from room to room. The coughs and whimpers floated through the halls from every room. And the smell—like formaldehyde mixed with cleaning solution. It hit my stomach like a brick.

No matter where I stepped, I couldn't get away from the darkness looming around every corner. The large building had so many corners and empty rooms, but I still couldn't find a place to hide. And worse still, the air pulsed with an aching sadness that tried to tear my heart right from my chest cavity.

But even among all the sadness, people still had hope gleaming from their eyes. Longing looks here, and faces tilted toward the sky in prayer there. Wishing and hoping for a better outcome, for a miracle. Still, the people must wait on the other side, staring at empty walls or closed doors while their loved ones rested just on the other side. Maybe if anyone bothered to give them any answers... but the staff was too busy for that.

That was me at the moment, except I couldn't sit still. Instead, I stood at the opening to the waiting room, my eyes not moving from the double doors that held her, my love, my life, on the other side. I needed someone to tell me what was happening, and my mind screamed with exasperation because I hadn't seen a single person leave that area. The doors hadn't even opened since they'd taken her in there.

Everyone else just sat together, talking or whispering. I even heard a few laughs, which only made me sneer. How could they laugh at a time like this? A time when we had no effing clue what was happening—or how our lives would change when someone finally explained the situation.

Our lives could be forever changed, and they were just sitting here acting as if nothing had happened. I had the urge to wrap my frail hands around their necks and squeeze, but that only made me think of images from a few short hours ago, so I quickly changed the course of my thoughts.

I had never been so petrified in my life. I knew what I saw would haunt my dreams for a long time. I still didn't know how I managed to pull her out of the blood red water. She'd cut herself again, carved words next to her tattoo using the blade I'd found beside her. I didn't know what they all said, but they were words of apology and love.

Words I'd rather have heard from her mouth than seen written on her naked body.

My mind couldn't process every detail of what I saw inside that bathroom. I hadn't looked in a mirror, but I could imagine how pale and sickly I probably looked. I sighed. I couldn't stand here anymore so I paced back and forth in the waiting room, but my mind replayed everything from the hotel, and I couldn't stop the reels in my head.

I could still feel her cold body against mine, so fragile, almost as if I moved her the wrong way she'd crumble into dust at my feet. Her blue lips made her pale skin look even more translucent, and my fingers had ghosted across them right before they took her from me. I had screamed and thrashed, only wanting her back in my arms, but someone had held me back. My mind was so hazy with anger and fear to recognize who it was. I couldn't even bring myself to care. All I cared about was the pale, unmoving figure lying still on the floor as paramedics worked her over.

"No!" I yelled again. "She needs me," I sobbed harshly.

I strained against the strong arms and kicked even more as they laid her on a stretcher and ra n out of the room with her.

"Lilith." I bolted forward with a river of tears streaming down my face. As I traipsed behind her, I had to wipe my runny nose.

I snapped back to the present as a tall figure blocked my vision of the nurses carrying Lilith down the hall. Strong arms gripped me again, pulling me back. A string of curse words flung from my mouth. I couldn't think of anything other than needing to be near her, holding her against me so she wouldn't leave me again.

I tried to focus through my tears, and I did enough to see disheveled bright blue hair, a tear-stained face, red lips, and an even redder nose. CG.

CG stood before me, looking at me with eyes so sad, they threatened to break me even further. I stopped fighting the person holding me. Or persons, I realized as I saw two sets of arms around me. When I turned, I found Jase and Jaxson, both of their faces shining with tears as well. I collapsed, giving up the fight and letting the sobs drop me to my knees. Instead of holding me back, their arms wrapped around me in comfort, forming a cocoon to hold each other.

"Lil..." I whimpered into Jax's chest.

"Shh. I know Alec. I know," his soft voice calmed my racing heart, even though his words cracked slightly.

CG joined our embrace, and we all sobbed as one unit, not knowing if our beloved fifth member would ever be here for another group hug.

The not knowing part would probably drive me to insanity. It had been four hours since Lilith was rushed to the hospital. Four agonizingly long hours of crippling fear and no answers. Not once had a nurse or doctor come to tell us what was happening or if she was okay. The minutes kept ticking on the clock, mocking me with every move of the handle. My eyes scrunched, releasing even more tears. I should have known there were more. I hadn't been able to stop crying, and I knew I wouldn't until someone told me something, anything, about her status.

"Alec...?" a soft, familiar voice asked from beside me.

My head lifted to see both my mother and Lilith's parents standing side by side with tears gathered in their eyes. I was moving toward them before I even had a chance to process they were here. I collapsed into my mother's arms, sobbing like a child who'd just fell and scraped his knee, and I called out Lilith's name repeatedly. She rubbed my back, soothing me in the way only a mother could. She whispered quiet things into my ear, none of which I could understand over my loud sobs, but her voice alone comforted me more than she'd ever know.

"Alec...sweetie, look at me." She pulled back, tilting my chin up. "It's going to be okay."

I rubbed my eyes. "Y-You don't know that Mom...we don't—they haven't told us anything!"

"I think what she means, Alec," Martha, Lilith's mom, said. "Is no matter what happens, it will be okay." Her swollen, red eyes seemed to tell a different story, though.

My eyebrows furrowed. She couldn't be losing hope already, could she? I hoped not, because if they all lost hope I would surely fall apart.

"How can you—how can you say that?" I rubbed the back of my neck. "She has to make it. She can't leave us. She can't leave *me*! I need her, Martha, I really do." I fell to my knees, my head in my hands, sobs wracking my body. I covered my face with my hands and tears poured through them. Everyone was watching, I was sure, but I didn't care. I'd been strong for so long, and I couldn't

"You saying stuff like that doesn't make it better. It's not your fault. If you want to put the blame someone, we're all at fault." She lowered her voice. "We all knew what this was doing to you both. We would have to be blind not to see it. You've both been miserable, and we all should have fought harder, should have said no, but we didn't."

"She did this because of me, CG." I couldn't look her in the eye, scared of what I might see shining back at me.

"No, she did this because *they* took *you* away from her. Not because of you, Alec. Because she couldn't have you, and she couldn't live in a world like that." She shrugged. "None of us know why she thought this would fix everything, but the fact is, Alec…I— I'm already dying inside. I mean, one of my best friends is in one of those rooms, being worked on by a team of doctors and I don't know if she'll ever wake up again. I don't need to hear anyone else saying they wish they were dead, okay?"

Jase came forward again, pulling CG into his arms. She didn't resist this time but instead wrapped her arms around his stomach and leaned into his chest. A pang of jealousy shot through me and I shook my head. What was wrong with me? I didn't need to be jealous right now.

As much as I didn't want to admit it, CG was right. I wasn't helping anyone by saying what I'd said. Nobody needed to hear it, so from now on, I'd keep my mouth shut.

"Rose?" a man called and all of us turned toward his voice in an instant. Lilith's parents, Martha and Nicholas, were on their feet and ran toward the doctor before I registered what had happened.

"How is she? Is she okay?" Martha asked, her words running together.

My mom pulled me to my feet. I stared at the doctor, who'd begun speaking quietly. Too quietly to hear anything. I wanted nothing more than to run up to them and listen, but somehow, I stayed back and gave Lilith's mom the respect she deserved. Just in case...in case she didn't make it.

Staying back didn't stop me from watching and analyzing every line of the doctor's face as he spoke. Martha's shoulders shook and my knees buckled, but I stayed on my feet. The doctor left Martha and Nicholas in shock with a hand covering their mouths. Murmurs of conversation flitted around me, but I couldn't hear them over the ringing in my ears.

She was *gone*.

My stomach lurched into my throat and I almost gagged. My head shook and tears fell like apples from trees onto my cheeks. Then my shoulders started to shake.

Martha turned, her eyes landing on me. My heart broke, knowing, but not wanting to believe. I would never get to hold her, touch her, kiss her, or tell her I love her again. We would never get to walk down the street, hand in hand, and declare our love for each other. I would never get to see her grow old and raise our children. Oh, how I had thought so many times about marrying her, having kids with her and seeing them grow and have our grandchildren.

If only I could go back in time. Retrace my steps to take me back to where it all began. To do some of it differently. To meet her bright eyes, red lips, and soft voice again. To see her play pranks and jokes on us. To see her adoration for her friends. To go back to all the times, we shared and make them last. And to go back to that day and fight. To fight like hell and never give up.

"Alec?" Nicholas, Lilith's father broke up my thoughts.

I cleared my tears away and eyeballed him, noticing his frown first.

"Did you hear what I said?" He put his hand on my shoulder.

I shook my head but already knew what his words would be. I didn't know if I was ready to hear them. Not yet. Not so soon.

But when he spoke, the world went dark around me and I almost fainted from happiness.

"She's going to be okay."

She's gonna be okay.

Chapter 13

Lilith

THE MIND WAS a dark and uncertain place, swimming with evil and greedy thoughts. Those thoughts wrapped around you and swallowed you whole, never letting up and never letting go. They take control of your body, rendering you speechless, motionless, and most importantly, powerless.

But that was what I'd wanted, wasn't it? To be rid of it all, to throw away my emotions, and finally be unguarded. Keeping up a guard, protecting myself, had turned into a difficult job. My head had strained so hard to keep the invisible wall up, not letting anyone else in. But sometimes, it became too hard to keep up and it slipped. Life turned a lot more dangerous then. Then people could get in. And that was when thoughts, ideas, and emotions crawled up your skin like a thousand spiders. It would fight relentlessly, not stopping until it took what it wanted. You.

It had me. Every piece of my body was covered in darkness,

floating through the black wind around me, and I couldn't see. My senses were severed, and I laid there as if I weren't there at all. Maybe I wasn't; maybe I finally did it. Maybe I had listened to myself and gave in to what I'd truly wanted. To die, to end, to stop.

But even in the haziness, through all the darkness and thick black clouds surrounding me everywhere, I could still see a light. It shone too brightly to ignore, and I couldn't look away even if I wanted. It captured my full attention and soon that was all I could focus on.

It was through that light I began to hear voices. Well, one voice. It broke through the wisps of black around me and fought for my attention. It screamed my name, but I couldn't see through the bright light encompassing it. I could swear my eyes were open and so were my ears, but I could only find bits and pieces of the voice.

"Lilith!"

That voice again, screaming my name over and over. Muffled cries came, too. Why was he crying? Had I done something wrong? The beautiful light darkened around the edges. I had a feeling if I didn't break out of the darkness it would pull me down, so I jumped up and tried to grasp the voice. My lifeline. I needed it to say more than my name. I wanted to know why I was here.

"No!" I screamed through my mind, but no real words came.

The edges thickened, caving in and blocking the light like a door shutting on it. I fought with everything inside me to reach it, to grab ahold of it, but it wouldn't stay. The emptiness in my stomach tightened as the light left me. I wanted to run toward it, but I couldn't. I wanted to scream, but I had no words. As the light disappeared with one final glint, I only had one tangible thought.

Game Over

Chapter 14

Alec

IT HAD BEEN two days since Nicholas had given me the news Lilith was going to be okay. Two days since I felt my world stop and start again all in one motion, and two days since I'd become angrier than I had ever been. I was caught off guard by my sudden mood change, but I understood it even if no one else did.

I knew I should be filled with happiness just like everyone else around me, but instead, I found myself breaking things and cursing my family. The moment Nicholas told me she was okay, I instantly felt at peace knowing she would live. I would get to see her again. Then I completely lost it. My vision turned red and hazy, and I ran out of the hospital faster than anyone could call my name.

A stream of calls and texts came in, but I ignored them all, taking a cab away from the hospital. I couldn't breathe anywhere near it and I didn't trust my anger being inside with everyone. I knew they expected me to be relieved because Lilith would make it, but I wasn't. No, now I was pissed off. I was angry at her and what she did.

How could she be so stupid? How could she have put us all through that?

As corrupted as it sounded, I wanted to break her, to hurt her. To make her feel exactly how she made me feel. I needed her to see what she'd done to me when she left me the first time and how broken I'd been when she tried to leave for good the second time. Did she think I would just be okay?

I yelled to the cab driver to take me to the one place I hadn't been in over a year. It hurt too much. Too many lost memories floated through every nook and cranny. Once, it had been filled with nothing but love. Now, only memories of that love had been stamped over every inch of it. I still felt it, somewhere deep inside me, but the hate had hidden it, shoved it down deep so I had to pillage to bring it back up. As soon as the cab pulled up to the curb, I threw money at the driver and slammed the door behind me, escaping the confines of the musty car. My long legs carried me quickly to the front. I wrenched the key from under the 'welcome home' mat and unlocked the door, halting just inside.

All the happiness I'd felt inside these walls had left me. Instead, my whole body shook with rage. I couldn't stop myself as I flipped the light on and stormed through the apartment, throwing everything from tables with a sweep of my hand and hurtling pictures at the wall. Glass shattered and fell to the floor, but it didn't stop me as I picked up a vase from the kitchen counter and held it over my hand and slammed it hard into the floor. Glass sprinkled my legs and fell under my shoes as I crunched forward, continuing my rampage.

My mind became numb as I turned over couches, broke TVs,

stereos, more pictures, and even the awards we had won as a band. Everything laid in shambles over the living room floor. I put my hands on my hips, taking it all in, and a cruel smile spread across my face. The happiness from the mess I'd created didn't last long.

"Damn you Lilith!"

I flung a bookshelf and frames splattered to the floor, books flew every which way. I moved forward and stumbled over my mess, so I kicked at it, clearing a path for my rage.

The kitchen: my next target. I rubbed my hands together and pushed forward, tossing pots into the ground and breaking glasses and plates over the floor. When I ran out of space on the floor, I tossed plates like Frisbees and shards of glass scattered down the wall. Hot tears streaked my face as I ran from the kitchen and up the stairs, my footsteps pounding into the ground.

I paused in front of the open room, peering into it and fighting all the memories crashing into my mind. It was her room, our room.

The place we once shared our love stood empty, bland, and cold. There was nothing to remind her of our time together. That pissed me off even more.

"You forgot me. How could you forget me?" I tore through the room like a hurricane, scattering music sheets and books as I went. I pounded a guitar into the ground, ripping everything to shreds.

"You didn't love me, couldn't have loved me. How could you do this? How could you try to leave me?" My throat hurt as I stepped to the corner of the room, finding the baseball bat Lilith always kept close by.

I gripped it and swung. I hit mirrors and pictures, not even looking at what I was doing. I didn't care. I just wanted her hurt to match mine, and it would as soon as she walked into her home.

"Why don't you want me?" I hit a homerun with a picture of Lilith and her parents in front of a large oak tree.

I cried even more loudly as I raised the bat to smash into the last picture, but stopped just short of hitting it. The bat dropped from my hands as though it had burned me, and I stared at the picture with an open mouth. It was us, Lilith and me together as we smiled happily, not caring who saw. Our love shined through our eyes as we latched onto one another fiercely.

I took a step back. At first glance, I hadn't seen a single picture of the two of us, but here it was. And I remembered exactly when we took it, days before she'd left me and broken my heart. A pain so intense it shattered me fell onto my chest. I'd never missed *us* as much as I did right now.

Jaxson found me shortly after I saw the picture. I was laying in the middle of the floor over a pile of glass, still holding onto the photo. He'd wrapped his arms around me, and I'd cried in his arms for hours, desperately wanting to understand why Lilith chose to do this.

***

She was still in the hospital and still asleep. The doctors said she had taken more than a handful of pills, and her lungs were filled with water. They thought she'd taken the pills before she got in the water so she could fall asleep in it and not struggle.

Nothing disgusted and hurt me worse than hearing the doctor say that. I wanted to believe he was lying, but I knew he wasn't. Lilith had known exactly what she was doing; she wanted to get the job done, and she'd taken measures to do so.

Today I felt like I could finally go to her room for the first time. Her mom, my mom, and the rest of the boys had already seen her, but I just couldn't. I'd had too much anger in me. I wouldn't have even been able to look at her. After the anger passed, my emotions swarmed me like a hive of bees, and I didn't want to disturb her rest. Today, though, none of that mattered. I had to see her. My body itched to be close to her, and I didn't care how messed up I was.

I walked down the long hallway, doors on each side of me. Some had patients inside, some with loads of family hovered around beds, and some were empty. The closer I got to her room, the more my heart sunk into my stomach.

My eyes fell upon the room number and her name listed below it. I clenched my eyes shut, my throat thick with tears. The image of the last time I saw her flashed across my mind. I didn't want to think about that right now, so I shook myself and squared my shoulders, taking in the new details, hoping I could get the drowning image of her out of my mind.

With a shaky hand, I turned the handle on her door and stepped into the dark room. The overhead lights were not on, but a soft glow came from a small bedside lamp. The beep from the heart monitor was the only thing I heard as I closed the door behind me, my eyes trained to the floor, afraid to look at her. My feet shuffled forward until I stood at the foot of her bed. The heart monitor beeped louder by the second.

Taking a few deep breaths, I forced myself to focus and my eyes slowly trailed up to her body. Small slim legs were hidden underneath multiple blankets that covered her all the way to her chin. Her frail, limp, and bandaged limbs lay loose beside her, unmoving. Her chest rose and fell with each breath, but they looked shallow, as if she were barely alive. As much as I tried to fight it, my eyes landed on her ghost-like face. I saw the breathing cannula in her nose, pumping more oxygen into her. She was probably too weak to get enough of her own.

Her soft, delicate features were hard to pinpoint past the pale and haunted look on her face. Her cheekbones stuck out so prominently, like sharp angles against a soft ground. I frowned. The rest of her bones looked much the same, all sticking out from her milky skin. If you weren't *really* looking at her, you'd never notice—like *I* never noticed.

"Oh, Lil," I whispered.

Had she not been eating? Had I been so blinded by jealousy I hadn't noticed? What was wrong with me?

With a few shaky breaths, I forced a calmness over me, making my way over to a chair next to her bed. My eyes found the bandages covering both arms from wrist to elbow. My heart stopped as I noticed the blood seeping through one of them.

I wiped at the tears that began to fall and reached over, my fingers still shaking as I picked up one of her ice-cold hands. It felt so limp in my hand. She didn't twitch. Didn't open her eyes. Didn't show any indication she knew I was here.

I let my head fall onto the bed, clutching both her hands now, as if she might disappear on me for good. My lips found her scarred left fingers, and I placed kisses along each of them. I wanted her to know I was here. That I'd never leave her again. Not now. Not ever.

"Why, Lil? Why did you do this?" I whispered. "Why didn't you just come talk to me? We could have worked this out together," I sobbed into her hand. "A-And now you're hurt. You're in here because of me...but...didn't you know how much this would hurt me?"

I bit my lip, then continued. "I've never stopped loving you, Lilith. *Never*. All I've ever wanted was to be with you, but I truly thought you didn't want me...and I—I don't know how I ever believed you didn't. I was so insecure, Lil...I thought maybe you could find better because you deserved better.

"But that doesn't mean I ever stopped loving or wanting you. It killed me every day to see you with him, and trust me, Lil, I know how you feel because I wanted to end it too. I wanted to get away because I couldn't stand to see you with someone else. Someone that wasn't *me*. But you know what? I couldn't do it. I couldn't take myself away from you even if I couldn't have you. I needed to be around you, even when we didn't speak. I still needed you...just to know you were there was enough."

I closed my eyes as tears streamed down my face. She probably couldn't hear me, but it felt good to get everything off my chest. It was easier now, since she couldn't respond and wouldn't be able to stop me.

"Am I not enough, Lil?" I softly spoke, glad she couldn't answer. "Is that why you wanted to leave me? I wasn't enough to make you want to stay even if you couldn't be with me? I still wasn't enough.... *I'm not enough.*" Hot tears rolled down my cheeks, falling to her hand and replacing the kisses I'd placed on them.

I had never been enough, and I still wasn't. I wasn't enough to make her want to stay and fight in the beginning, and now, I wasn't enough to make her want to continue breathing.

Lilith was the one laying in the hospital; she was the one who had tried to commit suicide and leave us. She'd been hurt, deeply hurt, by the events in her life and had been through things people should never have to go through. But what she forgot, what she still might not get, was even with what she was going through, someone else had been broken, maybe even more than her.

"You... are... enough, Alec. "

Chapter 15

Alec

"GO AWAY?" THE words slipped past my lips as my mind tried to wrap around the idea.

My heart refused to let Lilith more than ten feet away from me. It might make me crazy, but if it did, I'd be happy to live in that world. She could push me away. She could try to kill herself. But, she'd never get rid of me. I would always come running back to her. When you loved someone, that was just what you did. Nothing she ever tried to do would stop me.

"Yes, for a little while," my mom said sadly to me.

She rested her hand on my arm, rubbing it up and down like it would soften the blow. It didn't, not even close.

"But I—no, she—leave? Where? How long?" The questions spiraled from my mouth, not giving me a chance to even take a breath.

She didn't want to be the one to tell me this or explain what was happening. She didn't want to be the one to carry the burden and then pass it on to me, but she still did. Love and respect shined from her eyes toward me, but it did nothing to alleviate the pain swimming through my chest.

"I don't know how long sweetheart...until the doctors feel she's stable enough to come home."

"She is. She'll be fine. She just needs to relax for a few days is all," I argued.

She only shook her head. "You know that's not true, Alec." Her bottom lip quivered. "Lilith's sick, honey. She needs help, professional help, to bring her back from whatever dark place she's in right now."

"No," I snapped, yanking my body away as I stood up and paced back and forth in front of the table. "Nothing is wrong with her. She isn't sick, she's just shaken! I can help her through it, Mom. She needs *me*, not some stupid doctor."

She stood up, her wide eyes showing her shock at being yelled at by me, but I couldn't help it. Right now, she was a threat. She wanted to help them take Lilith away. I wouldn't have it. Not from any of them.

"You can't help her, Alec. She needs a medical team. She tried to end her own life, honey, she needs to be in a facility where—"

"Shut up," I yelled.

She flinched.

My body shook as I tried to take deep breaths, to calm my anger. I didn't want to yell at my mom. Not like this. Not ever.

Distantly, the door clicked open, but my eyes stayed trained on my mom.

"She doesn't need a damn facility! She needs to be with the people who love her and want to protect her." I stomped my foot like a petulant child who hadn't gotten his way.

"I get that, Alec, but you can't protect her from this." She met my stomp by placing her hands on her hips and giving me a pointed stare.

"Yes, I fucking can! Just give me the chance to."

I took a step toward her, and she stepped back. Somewhere in my mind, I knew my own mother was afraid of me and it scared me, but still, I didn't back down, couldn't was more like it.

"You already had the chance to, Alec, and look where she is now." As soon as the words left her mouth, she covered her lips with her hands, leaving only her wide eyes showing.

I deflated, like a balloon the air had been let out of. My mouth went slack as I stared at her, frozen, not sure how to react. When I snapped back to myself, I crumbled. My eyes fell to the floor along with my heart. My stomach flopped as her words hit me again, this time like a cannon knocking the wind out of me. I brought Lil to this place; I caused this.

"Alec, that's not what I meant." She lowered her voice, taking a step toward me. "I would never hurt you that way. I'm saying you can't protect her from everything. As much as you want to, you just can't. I know this hurts, but the best way to help her, to protect her right now, is to let her go. To get her the treatment she needs."

I closed my eyes, hearing her words, thinking about them, but still trying to fight them off.

"Alec."

A voice drew my attention to the corner of the room, and I took in a disheveled Martha, standing with her hands clasped in front of her. I lifted my head and met her gaze as she moved next to my mom.

"If she doesn't get the help she needs...she could try again and I—I can't watch my daughter go through this again. I can't take a chance and maybe lose her for good next time."

Her broken words pulled at my heartstrings. I nodded, taking in her shaking hands as they wrapped around herself. I felt the same, so I understood. More than she knew. It didn't change my mind completely. I still had reservations.

"I understand, really I do, but, I can't let her go again. What if—" All the air left my body in a rushed string of words. "What if she doesn't come back to me?"

"She will, Alec. I know her better than anyone else, and I know she will."

For maybe the millionth time since this began, my knees gave out all of a sudden. I barely fell into a chair right in front of two of the strongest women I'd met in my life. My mom came to me, wrapping her arms around my neck, and I buried my face into her chest. She whispered sweet, soothing words at me, but I couldn't hear them over my own moans.

I cried for Lilith and her loving personality, her sweet nature and her good soul. My heart broke for the girl I once knew and still loved with every fiber of my being. It shattered for the relationship we'd had, so broken it probably would never be mended. But most importantly, I cried because I didn't think I had the strength to carry on without her.

That night I was forced to go home by not only my mom and Lilith's parents but also the rest of the band. I, of course, put up a fight, but they wouldn't hear it. Instead, they forced me into Jaxson's car, and he drove me home. I made them promise to call if anything happened or changed, but I didn't think they would. The stress of the past few days rolled off me like a blanket when the temperature rose, making the tension around me so thick everyone choked on it.

Silence fell in the car on the drive home because I couldn't find anything I wanted to talk about. There were no light-hearted conversations to be had and talking about the current situation would only make everything worse.

Upon arriving at my house, Jaxson forced me upstairs and into the shower while he fixed me something to eat. I had been running on autopilot so much the past few days, I'd forgotten I needed to eat. My mind wouldn't stop repeatedly chanting Lilith's name. I couldn't get her out of my mind. I couldn't stop thinking about how this had all started. She'd told the story, and my mind had chosen tonight to try to process everything now that she was safe.

Ever since Lilith had broken things off with me I had been a mess. The first few weeks, I didn't leave my room unless I had to for work or was being pushed out by the others. No one spoke of what happened, knowing it would only make things harder. I barely slept, ate, or showered in those days, much less talked to anyone. I was stunned and heartbroken but mostly shocked. Lilith ignored me, of course, but I supposed maybe that helped in a way. Of course, now I wished she would have told me, but then again, would it have changed anything? Most likely not. She would still have been forced to sign a contract to break up with me, and I would have still been broken at the end of it all.

I would never forget how I felt the day she brought Markus home to meet us. I already knew that she and the boys knew him, but this was a different meeting; this was us meeting her new boyfriend. She walked, or more like waltzed, through the door with a smile on her lips and Markus's hand in hers. My stomach churned as soon as I saw them. I wanted to smack the happy looks right off their faces.

The band didn't know what to do, so they gaped at Lilith like she'd went crazy, but they didn't say anything. She just stepped into the room all fucking happy and greeted everyone in the room. Except me. No, she wouldn't meet my eyes, and that destroyed me.

"Guys.... this is Markus, my boyfriend," she had said.

The words left her mouth, and I jumped out of my seat on the couch, pushed past everyone and ran straight upstairs. I ignored their calls and remained in my room for another two weeks because I couldn't face either of them.

To me, he was everything she wanted and everything I wasn't. I wanted to be happy for them, and eventually I tried to be, but that only lasted a few days. I couldn't even act like I was okay with their relationship, and everyone knew it. I'd thought maybe my hatred for him and their relationship had nudged the final wedge in place between Lilith and I.

Sure, when we were out in public, we acted normal, but even then, I had a feeling people could tell I was acting a part. The light no longer shined from my eyes, but instead a beam of darkness covered everything I looked at. I couldn't act happy when I was so miserable, and people noticed. We ignored them and stayed in our little bubble instead. Only those on the inside knew what was really going on. But I hadn't even known there'd been a deeper secret involving Lilith, Markus, and Management.

All the thoughts raced through my mind as I stood under the shower head in my bathroom. I hadn't moved an inch since Jaxson had forced me in here, but now, he pounded on the door, so maybe I'd been in here too long. I finished my shower and quickly got dressed.

Heading downstairs to the kitchen, Jaxson stood perched against the counter with a plate sitting next to him.

"You need to eat." He handed me the plate with a sandwich and crisps on it.

"Yes, *mother*." I winked, earning a chuckle from him.

The table had been cleared, so I sat down and picked at my sandwich, eating a few pieces I pulled off. My mind still raced, and I couldn't shut it off as I stared at the dark wooden table. A sigh escaped from Jaxson as he sat down next to me.

"Eat, not play, Alec." He smacked at my hand.

I exhaled slowly, placing another piece of the sandwich in my mouth. It tasted like nothing and resembled cardboard as I chewed it, but I had a feeling it had nothing to do with the sandwich. I didn't want to eat. Couldn't care less about it.

More silence enveloped me as I forced myself to keep eating, to keep swallowing, and to keep thinking about everything I'd learned the past few days. There was one thing my mind kept hiccupping over, one thing I hadn't spoken to anyone about yet. Now, it poked at me until I couldn't keep it in.

"Did you know?" I asked.

"What?" He raised his eyebrows at me.

I planted my elbows on the table, folding my hands. "Did you know...about Lilith breaking up with me?"

"You mean did I know the real reason why?" he asked, and I nodded. He shook his head and rubbed his eyes with the palms of his hands. "No, I had no idea. I don't think any of us did."

"Jase did," I spat before I could think about it. My hands clenched a little tighter. "He knew the whole time."

"He didn't ask to know, Alec. You can't blame him." He leaned forward.

I rolled my eyes. "He knew, and he didn't tell me. He didn't tell any of us. He's my brother. Do you know how much of this crap would have never happened if he had just said something?"

"Alec, he was scared. Surely you can understand that."

"Not right now I can't because he gets to be happy with *his* girlfriend while mine is laying in a hospital bed." I slammed my elbows on the table.

"First off, Lilith isn't your girlfriend anymore, Alec, and that's not Jase's fault. He was protecting his relationship with CG. Do you really fault him for that? You're trying to tell me you wouldn't have done the same thing if the tables were turned?"

I sprawled back, kicking my legs out in front of me. His words stung. Lilith wasn't mine anymore, I knew that, but still, if she had been and the roles had been reversed, I would have done the same thing. It didn't take away the anger I had toward Jase. He should have told me. He was my brother, my family...he should have told me.

"Did you know they were together?" I changed the subject because if I didn't, my anger would consume me.

He shook his head again. "They hid it so well. But I'll admit, as shocked as I was...the two of them are kind of adorable together."

I flinched at his words. It shouldn't hurt me. I should be happy for them, but I missed being the adorable couple with Lilith.

I shrugged half-heartedly. "Yeah. I guess they are."

"They told you she's going away, didn't they?" he kept his voice soft, as if afraid to wake a sleeping dragon.

My hands stopped playing with my food and dropped to my sides as I gave a curt nod. An all too familiar ache settled into my heart again.

"It's the right thing to do, Alec."

"Is it? Because I kind of feel like the right thing to do is keep her here with me." I couldn't meet his eyes.

"Alec, I don't think you, or your relationship with Lilith, is the underlying problem anymore..."

I tilted my head at him.

"Your relationship may have been the start of all this, but somewhere along the lines it changed. Did you try to look past what she said about you in the Livestream? If you did, you might understand the real reason she did this." He shifted, stretching back and folding his arms over his chest.

"What the hell are you talking about? She talked about what happened to *us*. Why her life had been torn apart, and that happened when they made her stay away from me." My eyebrows scrunched on my forehead.

"Yes, that's true. But, look deeper than that, Alec. Look past all the relationship stuff and focus on what else she was saying. She's hurt from what they made her do, yes, but now it's become a crap ton of self-doubt and hate."

My mind reeled over his words.

He pushed on. "She said she didn't understand why she was brought into the group. Why we thought she was good enough because *she* didn't think she was good enough. Martin and Melissa used that against her and made her into their own personal puppet. Don't you see? She doesn't think she belongs here. If you were the entire reason behind all the pain she held inside, she would have come to you about it. She would have talked to you about it, and you would have brought it to us and then, maybe, we all could have helped her figure it out."

"So, what are you saying, Jax?" I held my breath, almost scared to hear the answer.

"I'm saying Lilith wanted to die because she doesn't think she deserves a place here anymore. She thinks we'd be better off without her."

I opened my mouth to respond, but the shrill ring of his phone cut me off. Jaxson reached over to the counter, picked up his cell phone, and answered it.

"Hello?" He mumbled a few "yeahs" and "okays" before hanging up the phone and looking at me.

"She's awake..."

I shot up from my chair so fast it fell back, slamming into the ground and ran to the hallway tugging on my shoes. Jaxson's loud footsteps followed me. Soon, he tugged on my arm, turning me to face him.

"Alec, wait."

"What? Let's go!" I turned to rush out the door, but he only grabbed my arm again. "Dammit, Jaxson, what?"

He sighed while pulling on his shoes and grabbing his keys. "They're getting ready to discharge her to the facility."

The frown found its way back onto my lips as he walked out the door, leaving me in the empty hallway staring after him.

She's awake but I'm going to say goodbye to her.

The drive to the hospital was slow, yet quick at the same time. My hands shook as I tried to figure out what I wanted to say to her. I also tried to prepare myself because she might not want to see me, which dug a hole through my chest, but it didn't make me expect it any less.

We arrived at the hospital, and I could see the front swarming with reporters and TV camera vans. I rolled my eyes and stuck close to Jaxson as we made our way past all the people shouting questions to no one in particular. We stumbled inside and made our way upstairs to see everyone standing outside Lilith's room.

CG and Jase stood off to the side together and looked up when we approached. Jaxson said his hellos and I greeted CG but I didn't look at Jase. He tried to say hello to me, but I just walked away. I was trying to not be angry at him, but it was so damn hard. I wanted to blame someone for this whole mess, and right now that someone was him.

I walked up to my mom and the corners of her lips perked. I leaned in, giving her a quick hug.

"What's going on?"

"Martha is in there with her right now. The doctors told her she's going to a treatment center, and she didn't take it very well. So, Martha is trying to calm her down and get her to understand." She straightened my jacket.

"Oh," I replied, not able to think of anything else to say. I slumped against the wall.

She rested her head against my arm and we listened to the quiet peace spreading through the hallway. The others huddled together, whispering to each other, but my mom and I were quite content waiting it out in silence.

About thirty minutes later, Martha stepped out, eyes rimmed red and walked over to the other boys, saying something quietly to them. They all nodded and walked inside Lilith's room, pulling the door shut behind them. I went to stand up straighter and follow them before I felt a small hand on my arm.

"Why don't you stay out here with us, Alec," Martha said to me softly.

I pinched my brows together. "What, why?"

She gave me a sad smile. "She wants to speak to them first." She fell into one of the chairs along the other wall.

My heart deflated. Maybe she really didn't want to see me. I could understand why, but I still didn't want to believe it. She couldn't leave without a goodbye. No, I wouldn't let that happen.

After another fifteen minutes and too much thinking, they came out and Jaxson walked over to me. He nodded his head toward Lil's room, and I lifted myself off the wall and walked to the door.

With a shaky hand, I turned the handle and walked inside. The beeping noise of the heart monitor was still the only sound in the room. The door shut with a thud as I stepped in. My eyes dropped to the small, fragile girl sitting up in bed, staring straight back at me.

"Alec," she said softly.

Stepping a little closer, I found myself at the end of her bed, not taking my eyes off her. She sighed, holding her thin, frail hands out in front of her, examining them.

"I'm um...sorry about earlier." She ran her fingers through her hair. "I was a little worked up I guess."

"It's okay." I shrugged, even though she wasn't looking at me, and I pretended to wipe something off my jeans.

"It's not, but whatever I guess. I just...I wanted to see you before they send me away." The last part came out a little bitterly.

I had to defend myself. "I tried to ask them not to, but they say you need it," I told her.

She shrugged and laid back in the bed. "Maybe I do. I'm not quite sure, my mind's a mess right now." She rubbed her forehead.

There were so many things I wanted to tell her, but my mind drew a blank, so I asked a question instead. "Why, Lilith?"

"Alec, don't..."

"No, Lilith. Why? Why would you try to do this?" I asked her again, not letting up, even though maybe I should.

"It's a lot more complicated than it looks," she replied.

"It doesn't have to be," I said. "If you had just told me, I could have helped. We could have done something. And we would still be tog—"

"No, Alec." She put her hand up, stopping me. "It would never have worked."

All the air rushed from my chest, and I couldn't breathe. It didn't stop me from rushing to her side and planting myself next to her on the bed. My palms covered her cheeks, and I lifted her gaze to meet mine.

"Don't say that, Lil. We were perfect, and you know that just as much as I do," I whispered.

"We may have been, but they wouldn't allow it." She tried to turn her head, but I wouldn't let her.

In that moment, everything that had haunted her the past three years shined in her eyes: the deep black darkness that had overtaken them, the hollowed out look in them, the fear and dread; I saw it all, and it hurt to look.

"I don't care about them or anyone else, Lil. I only care about you, about us—that's it. Nothing else matters if you and I are happy, babe." The nickname slipped out of my lips so easily even though it had been years since I'd said it last.

I saw tears well up in her eyes and slip down to her cheeks. My thumbs were quick to catch them before they could leave a stream on her beautiful face.

"I missed you," she breathed, and I felt the life crawl back inside of me.

A bright sun started to peek through the gray clouds when she'd said those words. A real smile found its way to my face.

"I missed you too. So much." I leaned my forehead against hers.

"I don't want to leave, Alec," she whimpered as more tears fell too quickly for my thumbs to catch.

I leaned in and whispered, "I know. But, you'll be back before you know it, and I'll be here waiting." Then I pressed a kiss to her cheeks to catch her tears while shushing her.

Her eyes searched my own, trying to find the truth in my words. I could tell when she found it because her eyes widened, and she grinned bigger than I'd seen in a long time. I meant every one. I'd wait for her. Forever, if that was what it took.

"Promise?" She leaned into my touch.

"I promise. I'll always wait for you. *Always*," I said into our quiet bubble.

She pulled back, staring into my eyes and then fell back against my chest. For a moment, a warm happiness spread through my chest, lighting me on fire. The weight of everything just washed away.

I might not have wanted Lilith to leave, but I knew it was for the best. She needed help. She needed to be reassured there were people who wanted her here. It killed me that she had to leave now, when I finally had her in my arms again, but to keep her safe, to make her whole again, I'd let her go.

I'd be waiting for the day she came back to me.

Chapter 16

Alec

THE DAYS AFTER Lilith went into treatment were long, dull, and boring. I tried to find things to do to keep my mind off her, but nothing worked. Worry seeped through me, eating away at me, and I felt like I was on my way to crazy town. I pictured different scenarios, some where doctors failed her and she ended up dead, and others where they fixed her and she came back to me as her old self. And then I'd think they'd locked her in a room just to get paid while they did absolutely nothing.

What if she wouldn't eat? What if she didn't get the medication she needed? What if they kept her away from any human contact and she went crazy? So many things could go wrong, and I couldn't do anything about it.

Deep down I knew none of my fake scenarios were true, but in my heart, I couldn't help but worry. I'd always felt like it was my job to look after her, even after she broke up with me. Sometimes we didn't speak, hell, sometimes we didn't have much of a relationship at all, but I could still check on her and see her. Even if we didn't say two words to each other.

And those thoughts led to my first mistake: not letting her know I was there with actual words. There were many more, too. My mind wouldn't let me forget any of them. I could have kept our friendship strong, then she would have known I was there for her. I could have opened up the lines of communication, reached out to her to tell her if she needed anything, I'd be waiting. Some might call me whipped, but I didn't care what they thought. I only cared what Lilith thought.

I wouldn't lie to myself, or anyone for that matter, and say I'd been a decent person for the last two years because I hadn't. I had said and done a lot of things I wished I hadn't, but those things had masked most of the pain. I wanted to show the world I was okay on the outside, though on the inside I was already gone. My heart had wilted, and I didn't want people to have to watch me suffer. Of course, I had no idea there were so many people in the world who'd enjoy the show. Maybe if I had, I'd have let them see my whole downward spiral into oblivion.

Instead, I hid it, and I hid it well. I drowned myself in parties, nightclubs, alcohol, and women. I kept it under wraps because I didn't need the media to catch ahold of it. Every now and then, they would catch me, and when they did, Jase always covered for me. I hadn't realized then how he must have pitied me, doing it out of guilt. I get it now, and I despise it.

It was so hard not to take my anger and my frustration out on him. I needed a scapegoat for this whole mess and he'd become exactly that, even though it had never been his fault. Sure, he knew about it and never told me, but I should have blamed myself.

I knew he had done what he did to protect CG. I understood it because I would do it for Lilith in a heartbeat, but I also felt betrayed. He'd let me fall through the cracks so he could save his own relationship. He said he'd done it to protect me, but in my eyes, it was his own selfishness that had pushed him forward.

He knew how torn up I'd been. He knew I'd been partying, could see the pain in my eyes, and yet he kept his secret.

What was hard to reconcile, however, was the fact that Jase's kind heart had always been loyal. He'd been there for me, even more than Lilith had been. Sure, he was my brother, but he was also my best friend. He betrayed me, and in doing so, he helped me; even when I tried to ignore him, he stayed at my side. Always there for me.

The way he looked at CG and the way that CG looked back...I shook my head as I pictured it. The love and passion they shared for each other was apparent in their eyes, and its strength could bring me to my knees. I'd felt the same thing once and still craved to feel it again.

When that thought hit me, all my anger toward Jase disappeared. I could never fault him for loving someone so much he would do anything to keep her safe.

The weeks started passing faster, but my worry grew more and more. I'd chewed my nails so much they'd bled and dark circles coated my eyes. My heart hurt more than it ever had before.

Everyone, and I mean everyone, had heard from Lilith. They'd received a letter, an email, or a phone call from her. She told them about her treatment and how it'd been helping her. She explained she still had issues, but her doctor believed things were getting better. She'd started to gain weight and no longer refused food. The battles in her mind still waged, but she was working through them in deep discussions with her therapist. All in all, she was getting better. She wouldn't be coming home yet, but soon. They were all so happy to hear from her.

Everyone but me.

She sent me nothing. No email, letter, and not a single damn phone call. Every time the mail came, I yanked it from the carrier's hands. I checked my email and call logs every ten minutes. Nothing. I thought maybe she erased my email, forgot my address, or didn't take my phone number with her.

I tried to reach out to her but still received nothing. She never replied to my letters, emails, or constant string of calls. Anytime I would mention it to my family or the others, they would just say "Soon, Alec," but nothing ever came.

Weeks turned into months of treatment. The rest of the band and I were kind of at a standstill with our career, not only because we didn't have Lilith with us, but because we had big decisions to make regarding our management team.

It was difficult without Lilith's vote, but not impossible. We just had to act on her behalf as best as we could. And with what she'd gone through, it wasn't as hard as it might sound. We were all furious knowing what they did to her and couldn't imagine keeping the same management team. So, we fired them.

Words were thrown, lawyers brought in, and contracts thrown out, but we didn't back down. There was no chance in hell any of us would work with them again after what they'd done

Things got harder each day. Lilith was still a part of the band, and we couldn't do much except for the occasional interview without her. The rest of the tour had been canceled; premieres, signings, everything. While we had to deal with a lot of pissed off people, we couldn't bring ourselves to do anything without Lilith. In a way, she'd become the face of the band. She was the lead singer after all. It wouldn't be right trying to find someone to fill in when the original would be better in a short matter of time. Music could wait. Her life could not.

Our career wasn't the only thing taking a dip without her. So were our personal lives. No one had the motivation to do anything. We should have been getting stronger and pulling together, preparing for when Lilith came home, but instead we drifted further apart.

I holed up in my house and didn't leave unless forced. My anger had dissipated, but it was still too hard to look at the love between CG and Jase. And then Jaxson, mumbling how adorable they were all the time...I couldn't take it so I shut myself in. It might not be fair, but I couldn't breathe around them. I just needed to be alone.

In the first few weeks after Lilith left, we watched all the news and media outlets we could, curious to see how the fans were taking the Livestream—and everything else that followed. They weren't taking it well, at all. They were sad and hurt. Some of them felt like they hadn't appreciated her enough. Some felt like they put too much pressure on her. And others threw the blame around, mostly toward me. I knew the need to blame all too well, so I took it, but it still stung, leaving a festering welt in my soul.

The ones that blamed me said I hadn't gotten to her fast enough that night. I didn't deserve her then, and I sure didn't now. They wanted me to leave. For good. Part of me accepted it as true, but I couldn't make myself leave. I made a promise to Lil to be here when she came back. If she wanted me to go then, I would. But not until she told me to.

Fall had come and the leaves had started to change into beautiful yellows, oranges, and reds. It was normally my favorite time of year. There was just something about the crisp air, the smell of dried leaves and seeing so many pumpkins out that made me smile. I loved walking down the street, kicking the occasional leaf around, and enjoying my time outdoors. Now, doing it gave me too much time to think. October may have brought new weather, but it hadn't brought me any happiness.

All the years of enjoying fall had come to a halt as I walked around with emptiness filling me up. The colors weren't bright anymore, and the air made my throat so dry I couldn't swallow. Nothing stood out to me. Nothing put a smile on my face. Everything moved and swayed, but with no extra life. No extra zest, and it made it all seem dull and completely uninteresting.

Some fresh air had sounded good. I thought maybe it would help me clear my head, but even as I counted the cracks in the sidewalk, my mind didn't slow. Had I stayed home, I would have had my mom or the guys nagging me to do something, eat something. and I didn't want that either. So, I ended up walking along the sidewalk, with no idea where I wanted to go. Now, I regretted that decision as the loneliness creeped up my spine, more than when I stayed home and hid.

Three months had passed and I hadn't heard a word from her. Three fucking months. Though letters and phone calls kept coming in, not one had come for me. Even my own twin brother had received a letter from her, but not me, the one who loved her more than anyone. I thought when she left we were okay. I thought everything would be fine and it would all go back to normal, but clearly, she'd had other ideas. I kicked the ground, wondering if maybe I'd said or done something wrong to change her mind. She'd left that day with a sweet kiss and a soft tearful goodbye from me, but she'd made a promise that she'd come back. I made one, too. I'd be here waiting.

Everything had turned to crap.

I missed her more and more as each second ticked by, and I grew anxious to see her. The anger crept back in. I hated that she hadn't contacted me and worried she didn't love me.

I sighed as I realized this stupid walk had done nothing to calm my nerves, but instead, added to them. With a shrug, I turned and began the walk back home, preparing myself to deal with the ambush of people waiting outside. The fans wouldn't leave, no matter what I said to them.

Sounds, smells, people all passed by in a blur, and I paid no attention to anything. I was on autopilot all the time and it barely got me through the days. My head lifted as I approached the house and heard the lid to my mailbox open. My heart used to flutter at the sound, hoping for something for me, but now it sounded like nothing more than a dull thud.

The mailman gave me a soft smile before handing over the small stack of envelopes. I thanked him and turned to walk up the steps and into my house while sifting through the mail, rolling my eyes at the junk addressed to me. I almost tossed everything in the trash bin when I saw one envelope written out to me in delicate and beautiful handwriting.

This time, my heart did flutter, and I thought it might have skipped a beat as the letters tumbled from my hand. All but one. I read the sender's name over and over.

Lilith Rose

A soft gasp escaped my lips. She had finally sent me something. My mind raced as my hands tore at the envelope, ripping out the small sheet of paper inside. My face broke into a smile as I thought about all the words she could have written me, telling me how much she missed me. I could already see myself writing out a speedy reply to her so she would know I hadn't left her. My hands shook as I unfolded the letter and stared down at it. My eyebrows knit together in confusion at the blank and empty page. No long words of love. Nothing about how much she missed me. I scanned it again, turning it over, thinking maybe I'd missed something. My mind raced, searching for answers that would probably never come as I read the two words neatly written on the back of the paper.

I'm sorry.

Chapter 17

Lilith

Day 1

LEAVING THE HOSPITAL could have been the hardest thing I have ever had to do, but having to say goodbye to my family and closest friends, all the people I loved, was definitely the single, most difficult thing I'd ever done. I tried not to put up much of a fight, but my insides screamed for them not to let me go. My skin crawled at the idea of a treatment center. The words tasted bitter on my tongue and burned my lungs. I didn't want to take a step near the place, but I had no choice.

Even though I refused to go, the doctor's order overruled my decision. I had to go a facility to seek treatment for what I'd done. Fine then. I would.

It had all seemed so silly to me at first. But then they used words like suicide-watch and self-harming. The reasons I had to go made sense then, even though I still refused. I yelled at anyone who told me I didn't have choice. I kicked and screamed and pushed everyone away. I begged and pleaded to all of them to let me stay. In my head, I didn't need help. I was okay. But they could tell I wasn't.

What made me stop were the words my mother brokenly whispered to me. She tried everything she could to calm me down, but her words didn't soothe me like they used to. Because now they held a threat to send me away, so I recoiled from them. But when she brought my father into the conversation, I stopped.

Just thinking of the pain that was so obvious in his eyes, the words he'd said to me, made me rethink everything. After that, my mom explained her true fears if I didn't go. She didn't want me to hurt myself again. To lose it with nobody there to save me next time. I could have explained her fears were unprecedented. I knew in my heart I would never attempt to end my life again, but I also knew things could change in a matter of seconds.

The hardest person to say goodbye to had been Alec. I wanted to wrap myself around him, bury myself in him like I was a butterfly inside a cocoon and never, ever leave. I wanted to smell him, to feel his warm arms around me and to stay right there, with him, for the rest of my days. I hadn't been comforted by him in so long. We hadn't even spoken in forever. Not on our own terms. And I had to leave him. Again.

He tried to hide it, but I could see my imminent departure tore him apart, limb from limb. His eyes couldn't hide a pain so deep it made my stomach churn. I almost asked him to take me away. Just him and me, no one else, and certainly no treatment center. But then an image flashed across my mind. Me, sitting in the bathroom, a bottle of pills in my hand. Pouring five, ten, twelve into my hand, and pouring them down my throat. I didn't know how many I took, but it had been enough to ensure I wouldn't survive. A sour taste coated my throat as I thought about my stomach lurching to rid itself of the pills, and me, swallowing through it, keeping them all down. Finally, I saw myself turning the water on and laying back, waiting for the pills to pull me into a deep, deep sleep. One I would never wake up from.

I couldn't stand that he had been the one to find me. He'd probably never be able to get that image out of his head. Not for the rest of his life. No, I could never do that to him again, to any of them again, so I would do whatever it took to get better. I would go to a facility. I would listen to the doctors and sit down with a therapist. I would get better, not only for myself, my family, and the band; but for him, too. I would get better for him.

***

Week 1

This was complete and utter bull. They treated me like I was completely insane. Someone watched me everywhere I went. Even when I had to use the restroom, the door had to be open and they stood right outside. The people here breathed down my neck, never took their eyes off me and gave me no space. Whatsoever.

"You're at risk to hurt yourself again, Lilith."

"It's just a precaution, Lilith."

A precaution against what? I couldn't get my hands on anything I could use to hurt myself, or anyone else, in this building. So, why did they have to be up my ass?

I needed to get out of here, and I looked for ways, but found nothing. Then I was frustrated and needed an outlet for it, which used to be me cutting myself. But here, I had nothing, so I swallowed it down and buried it until I could deal with it. But I was sick of it all.

I wrote letters to everyone back at home. I called and begged them to get me out of here, to let me come home, but every single time I got the same answer: "It's what's best for you."

How the hell would they know? Were they here? Nope. So, they couldn't know what was best for me...

I felt like any minute I might suffocate. Maybe if I did, it would end my suffering. I could imagine every breath leaving my body until I could take no more. If I succumbed to it, maybe I wouldn't be so damn miserable. Maybe I wouldn't be so damn lonely. Maybe I just wouldn't be.

Loneliness. It was the worst part of this. I missed him, *needed* him. But he'd already forgotten me. He didn't reply to any of my letters. He didn't write me any emails. Nothing. I guess I deserved it, him leaving me. After all, I left him first, or tried to.

I want to die.

***

Week 4

I was *numb*.

A numbness had settled over me. Everything around me, all the feelings I used to have, left me dead inside. There were no more bright colors. They were all dull. Nothing tasted good, it just...tasted like nothing. And everything around me had no meaning at all.

Every day, I sat on my bed all and stared at the blank wall until an orderly wearing white scrubs came to get me, which they only did when it was time to eat or time to sit with my therapist. There were plenty of things to do here; they hadn't locked me up in a prison, but I didn't have the motivation to do anything but sit in my room, staring at my wall. It took the pain away. Staring at nothing. Because *I* was nothing.

No one visited. The letters came, but not as often. I got an occasional phone call, but no more than a five-minute conversation. Tops. And my inbox had been empty for weeks. I'd learned to stop caring.

Except when I thought about Alec. I couldn't understand why he wouldn't reply to me, and it hurt. Thinking about him was the only time I didn't feel numb, and he forgot me. I'd thought at first he was slow, or he got busy with things at home. Now, I couldn't make excuses. He didn't want me in his life, not even to speak to me. He wanted nothing to do with me.

Who could blame him, though? I left him. For two years. After claiming I loved him. Then I treated him awfully, like I had risen above him. Like he was no more than an old piece of gum stuck to the bottom of my shoe. I thought I had to do it. I thought making him think the worst of me would make him stay away. But, obviously, it killed a part of him.

Now, I could never fix the mistakes I made. My life would forever lay in ruins at my feet, and I couldn't build it again. I'd ruined our past and destroyed any chance at a future. Now I had no one.

"So, Lilith, how do you feel today?" Nicole, my psychiatrist asked, tapping her pen on her notepad.

I feel numb.

She dipped her chin, peering over her glasses at me. "Honestly, Lilith."

I sighed heavily. "You know what, Doc? I'm not sure if I'm depressed or not. I mean, I'm not exactly sad, but I am not exactly happy either. I can laugh and smile, joke around with the other patients, but sometimes at night, when I'm alone, I forget how to feel." I gave her the truth for the first time since coming here, and I could tell by the look in her eyes she knew it.

"Do you know what we call this, Lilith?" she asked. "*Progress.*"

I got up not feeling like I made any progress at all.

***

Week 8

Things had gotten better after my confession last month. The pain still sank into my chest, but it had morphed into a dull ache. My sessions continued regularly, and it became easier to cope with everything that happened. I opened up to my shrink and talked about my anxiety, fears, and desire to die. It had been a slow process, but eventually, we weeded through my insecurities and got down to the root of the problem. I wasn't okay yet, but I was well on my way.

I talked about how much I missed my family, my friends, and even my fans—if they were still there. The letters had all stopped, so I had no idea what, if anything, had happened at home. At first, I'd been angry, thinking everyone had given up on me, but my doctor opened my eyes. They were giving me space. The space I needed to heal. I believed almost everything Nichole said, and she helped me work through so many things. Now, I could finally smile without forcing it.

There were phone calls occasionally, to check in, but they were short. I'd get down again afterward, but my doctor would help raise me back up, reassuring me my friends were there for me, they just wanted me to have the time I needed. It made me happier and put me in a better place.

I no longer sat on my bed and stared at the wall. Instead, the minute I woke in the morning, I hopped to the rec room and got lost in the piano there. I even went to a group therapy session and learned all sorts of things about other people. It opened my eyes even more and helped me with own issues.

Reading also helped me. Getting lost in a fantasy novel, which I never thought I'd like, helped pass the time. I sat on my bed with the newest novel I'd been given to read. I had an hour until dinner, and then a session with my therapist. I felt the need to relax before my busy evening.

I was just getting into the deepest part of my book when I heard a light tap on my door. I lifted my eyes as a plump nurse with bright red hair stepped in, giving me an easy smile.

"How are you feeling, Lilith?" she asked.

I smiled and nodded at her, letting her know I felt fine.

She came closer. "There's someone here to see you."

I straightened, setting the novel on the bed. "Who?"

She shrugged. "Not sure, but they've been cleared to have half an hour to visit with you."

I gave her a genuine, bright smile and hurried out the door, my heart fluttering with excitement.

People smiled and greeted me, but I didn't slow down. No, I raced, and my heartbeat sped up, thumping so loud I could hear it. I had no idea who could be here. It might be my mom, CG, Jax...or maybe even *him.* But I tried not to get my hopes up.

When I reached the rec room, I took long strides all the way to the far corner where round tables were set up for visitors. Other patients already sat there, laughing and carrying on with family or friends.

I scanned the area, my eyes landing on a man perched on one of the chairs. He looked around, and my eyes widened. I remembered everything about him. My stomach flip-flopped as I stopped in front of the table.

The air left my lungs in a whoosh as I drank him, gulping.

"Hi, Lilith."

I'd never forget that musky voice. My throat constricted and I struggled to swallow. I had given up all hope that anyone would come visit me. I believed what the doctor said. They were giving me time to heal. So, I pushed aside those hurt feelings, grateful they thought so much of me to give me the space I needed. Now, standing here, I got lost in a sea of confusion.

"*Markus?*"

Chapter 18

Alec

IT HAD BEEN six months since Lilith left. Six months of loneliness, bitterness, sadness, and silence. Every passing day left me with so many questions. How was she? Had she improved? Was she getting better? Did she still love me? All the letters, phone calls, and now even video chats the others or our families received didn't answer those questions because I didn't get the answers from Lilith. I had started to think I never would.

Even after all these months with no word from her, I still sent her letters every day. Sometimes they were short, and sometimes they were long and filled with pain and sadness because lately, that seemed to be all I had left. The emptiness had disappeared the day I said goodbye to her, but now it had come back with a vengeance. And only she could fix it.

Everyone around me tried to comfort me, but I shut them out, all of them. I didn't want to hear their sympathy or their words of encouragement. To me, they were all bull. They could say they knew

163

how I felt all day long, but they didn't. The person they loved the most in the world hadn't turned their back on *them.* They still saw their loved ones every day, heard from them, texted them. Whatever. I didn't.

The pain had started when I didn't hear from Lil for two weeks, but it had only been in my heart. Now, it spiraled out of control, wracking my whole body. It didn't matter if I stood, walked, sat, or laid down, I was in pain. Always. People used to tell me emotional pain could never really hurt. I chuckled to myself. Boy, were they wrong. I couldn't even breathe right now without it hurting.

I started to understand why Lilith had wanted to end her life. Those dark feelings swirled through me now, starting deep in my core and festering through my mind and soul, like a disease that had no cure. They attacked my thoughts and sliced through my desires until I could almost taste them on my lips. It overwhelmed me, but at the same time, it could be so very peaceful.

I was barely hanging on. And only one thing would change that. I wanted Lilith back. I *needed* my Lilith back.

Seven months and eight days into Lilith's treatment, we each received a phone call from Martha: *Lilith was coming home.*

I was lying in bed, staring at the ceiling, when I got the phone call. As soon as it ended, I looked around, seeing everything clearly for the first time. I came to terms with the fact she'd be back in two days, but I didn't know how to prepare for her return. I had no one left. I'd turned everyone away. They tried to stick with me but eventually gave up. But, Lilith needed a welcome home party—or I at least needed someone to jump up and down with her.

Pushing everyone away hadn't made me feel lonely. Their absence hadn't affected me. Not like Lilith's silence. Every second, minute, hour went by like a knife stabbing my cutting my chest, slicing deeper each time.

The faint sound of a door opening found me lying on the bed. I didn't move, and the band walked in, smiling as if nothing had happened. I smirked, amazed that even though I'd told them to forget me, they never would.

"Hey..." Jase said, hesitating a little.

Out of all of them, the anger I'd felt had hit him the hardest. Even though I'd come to realize a while ago nothing had been his fault, it had taken me awhile to get rid of my anger. He'd done what he did for Lilith. Maybe I was jealous, of course, I'd never admit it to him.

"Hey," my voice cracked. I hadn't used it in months, or close to it.

As a unit, they took a deep breath and stepped into the room. I took them all in, the protective stance Jase had beside CG, and her glancing at him every few seconds, probably making sure he still had a smile on his face. Jaxson stood with his shoulders wide and legs wider, confident, collected on the outside. But, his eyes held a deeper emotion I couldn't quite name. I'd missed my best friends. And as soon as the thought crossed my mind, I wished I could go back in time and never put them through what I did.

"Jesus, Alec, it smells really bad in here," CG coughed as she sat next to me. "And so do you." She pinched her nose, giving me a playful smile.

"*Chloe*," Jase gazed at her carefully and looked back to me.

I smiled and shook my head. CG's jokes were exactly what I needed right now.

CG pressed her lips together. "I know...sorry."

I cleared my throat. "I'm guessing you heard, and that's why you're here?"

Nods and smiles came from each one of them. Jase and Jaxson sat on the end of my bed while CG opened the window to let in some fresh air. Then, she made her way over to me and pushed on my shoulders, forcing me to sit. She came down right beside me.

"Martha called you?" Jase asked, and I nodded. "She called each of us too."

"Yeah, and interrupted some extreme bonding if you get what I mean." CG winked at Jase.

A blush crept up Jase's neck and spread to his cheeks. I burst out laughing, and everyone else followed. I laid my head on CG's shoulder, smiling. I had been missing a single person so much I pushed all the people in this room away, but I needed them. Having them in my life made so much of the pain fade. Made it easier to breathe. I don't know what I'd been thinking.

I folded my leg under me. "So, when does she arrive?"

"Martha said she's picking Lilith up and bringing her back to her place. They've already gone through her house and put some safety precautions in place, but her doctors say she's done amazingly well." Jaxson's huge grin looked odd against his serious features.

I grew quiet and fiddled with the blanket under me. I let a sigh escape and nodded.

"Alec, you know there has to be a logical explanation, right? Lilith would never just exile you like that," Jase said.

"She did, though." My teeth bit into my bottom lip, and a lump hit the back of my throat.

"Well, I don't believe that for one minute. I mean, come on Alec. It's Lilith," CG admonished.

They all nodded in agreement, and I tried to make myself think as they did. I tried with all my might, but deep in my gut, I had a sinking feeling. Something didn't feel right.

"I guess we'll see."

After a few hours catching up with the guys, they all lectured me about my health and made me get out of bed. Much to my protests, I was thrown into the shower to wash the stink away while they set about cleaning up my long-neglected apartment. To say it was disgusting would be an understatement.

A few bottles of cleaner, a lot of trash bags, and gallons of fresheners later, my apartment smelled fresh and clean again. They ordered pizza and sprawled out in my living room to watch a movie. I sat down next to Jaxson on the couch and joined them, enjoying being around others for the first time in months.

"I say we throw a coming home party," CG said, breaking the silence after a while.

I raised my eyebrows at her.

"Is that a good idea? I mean, after everything she's been through? Would it be too much, too soon?" Jase asked his girlfriend.

Girlfriend. It would take some time to get used to calling her that.

"Well, the doctor did say it's best if Lilith goes back to her normal life but stays away from stress for a while. What's a better way to celebrate her recovery and return home than a party with her friends and family?" CG responded.

"I have to agree with Jase. We don't want to overwhelm her," Jaxson added.

I could only sit there quietly because quite frankly, I knew nothing about what was going on with Lilith right now.

"Well, how about just a few people then? Just us and Lilith's family?" CG asked, her eyes glimmering with hope.

I shrugged, looking at Jase and Jaxson who both mimicked my movement.

"Sure, babe," Jase, and CG grinned as she snuggled into his side. He planted a kiss on her forehead and rested his head against hers.

"You two make me sick," Jaxson groaned, chucking a pillow at them.

I laughed. Hard.

"You're just jealous," CG bellowed through her chuckles, throwing the pillow back.

Jaxson caught it midair.

I smiled to myself as they bantered back and forth. When Lilith came home, everything would be normal again. And I couldn't wait.

Two days passed quickly, and I was ready to see my girl. I woke up smiling for the first time since she'd been gone. I was ready to face the day, to have Lilith back in my arms.

Nothing else mattered. I forgot about the lack of letters and not having any contact with her, and I focused on the fact she'd be home today. I met up with the band at Lilith's apartment, and we hung streamers and signs. CG's idea, of course. She planned the whole thing. Next to me, I didn't think anyone was more excited than Chloe-Grace. Lilith had always been her best friend and one of her favorite people. They laughed when they were together and never stopped smiling, which meant I wasn't the only one freaking out right now. That helped.

My hands shook so hard I knew I wouldn't be much help, so I paced in front of the window instead. The guys tried to give me simple tasks, but I'd spill something or tear something. They eventually banished me to the living room to wait it out. My nerves were on overdrive, and they were getting the best of me. I couldn't stop staring at the clock, but it didn't make the hands move any faster. I might have had a few patches of hair missing since I couldn't stop pulling on it.

"Alec, calm down, they'll be here soon," Jase said while he set out some drinks for everyone.

I sighed and started to pace again. "I know it's—I—I'm so damn nervous! What do I say when she gets here? Do I hug her? Am I allowed to kiss her? What do I do?"

He knew I wasn't angry at him, so he just smiled and held back a laugh. The sudden sound of car doors opening and slamming shut made their way inside, and I looked outside with wide eyes.

"I guess you're about to find out." Jase smiled and opened his arms for CG as she bounced back into the room.

"They're here!"

Her announcement, even though I'd already seen them pull in, made my body shake even more. I had no idea what to say or do around her now. I didn't want it to be awkward or different; I wanted everything to be like it'd been before. I needed our old connection. I wanted to take her in my arms and kiss her until she couldn't breathe, and after I did that, I wanted to lead her to her room and show her exactly how much I'd missed her.

My pain had vanished this morning. Despite all the nerves, I was finally happy. I was able to look past the hurt I'd felt. It could never compare to Lilith's pain. Everything had led us here, and I made a promise to myself: I'd be whatever Lilith needed me to be right now. I'd be strong for her, fight her battles for her, whatever she needed. I only wanted to see her happy.

I was prepared to do anything for her, to lay everything down, quit the band, and just be there for her. Anything at all she would ever need. But, I wasn't prepared when she walked in, hand in hand with someone else. Someone that wasn't me.

I wasn't prepared for when she walked in with *Markus.*

Chapter 19

Alec

I PULLED AT the collar of my shirt, unable to pull in enough air. It could be because the walls were closing in around me. I couldn't find any words, but I didn't think any were needed. I stood frozen, not sure what to do, but not able to move an inch. What was she doing here with him?

A cold shiver climbed up my spine. Not from nerves. No, they were gone, replaced with a bone-deep ice tracing around my heart. The cold continued, biting my arms and chilling my fingertips. I felt like if I touched anything, it would turn to ice.

The room started to spin around me, and my grip on reality wavered. My instincts screamed at me to charge forward, to claim Lilith as mine. My brain cut in, reminding me this wasn't the Stone Ages, and even if I wanted to, my feet were planted in the ground. I stared straight ahead, never taking my eyes from their intertwined hands. I flinched. Never had I thought I'd see them together again, and here they were—right in front of my face.

I wouldn't meet their eyes, didn't even risk a glance at their faces. If I did, it would be over. If they smiled at me or acted like they were happy, I'd snap. They'd ruined me once; I wouldn't let them again.

There was no way this was a coincidence, and she didn't have Management threatening her behind closed doors this time. She wanted this. She'd chosen it. Fine. But this time, I wouldn't let it break me.

"Um...Lilith?" CG stumbled forward, her mouth slightly parted.

My eyes hadn't moved from their hands. The bigger one kept squeezing the smaller one, and every time my hands clenched. When my nails dug into my palms, my body welcomed the pain, it kept my mind on something other than the two standing in front of me.

"Hi, everybody." Lilith's cheerful voice echoed through the room.

I winced. She sounded like her old self. Happy. Free. Full of joy, and here I stood, the exact opposite of every one of those things.

"This is, uh, well, Markus?" Lilith's voice wavered when she said his name. But only a little.

When the name left her lips, I wanted to punch the wall. I still hated him. It didn't matter how much time had passed. I never would like him. I'd always hate him, but probably never as much as I did right now.

He gave a corny wave. "Hi."

"What, no hugs, or 'Welcome Home' for me?" Lilith asked, her voice turning high-pitched.

Just like that, everyone snapped out of their funk and leaped forward, wrapping their arms around Lil and enveloping her in a group hug. I didn't move an inch.

Just like old times only this time I wasn't in there.

I stopped staring at their hands and took in the group, huddled around each other, smiling and talking, congratulating Lilith on her recovery. Sloppy kisses were even thrown around. Her eyes gleamed as she took them all in. This moment would have been perfect if it weren't for the tall guy hovering behind Lilith with a smirk on his face. It would be even better if he weren't directing that smirk at me.

The insides of my palms began to ache as my nails dug deeper and deeper. The glare calcified on my face as I stared at him and saw the wheels turn in his head. He didn't look away or back down. Everyone around us was so oblivious to the war being fought in the middle of Lilith's living room. I clenched my jaw so hard my teeth clacked together. Lilith chose that moment to meet my gaze and offered a small wave.

"Douchebag," I muttered to no one else but myself.

"Alec?" Lilith questioned, my name falling off her lips like a flower blooming in the sun. Beautiful.

I didn't let her pretty voice deter me. "Lilith," I nodded at her curtly.

Wrinkles broke out on her forehead. Was she stunned? How could she be? I wanted to laugh at her reaction. What did she expect? The way she'd left me with so much hope in my heart; then she arrived with *him*. Of course, I wouldn't be happy.

"It's uh...nice to see you." She looked at her feet.

"I'm sure it is.," my voice could have frozen Costa Rica. I looked at the others, but they offered no support. Instead, they pleaded with their eyes for me not to make a scene.

I wanted to grab hold of her, to shake some sense in her, but I couldn't. I knew that. She'd made so much progress. It was etched all over her face.

When she left, she'd been the most unhappy and unhealthy she had ever been. Now, she looked great. There was more color to her now filled-out face. No longer did dark circles rim her eyes, they were bright, just like the ocean, again. They still took my breath away. When I stared into those eyes, everything else dissipated. The anger fell away. I wanted to help her, even now. To make sure she had everything she needed. It couldn't be about me. Not now. It had to be about her and what was best for her.

So even though I would have liked nothing more than to battle my enemy and claim what was mine, I knew it would ruin every bit of progress that Lilith had ever made.

It was at this moment I truly understood what unconditional love was. It was sacrificing my own needs for the one I loved. It was putting every want or hurt aside and only focusing on my other half. It was letting go when I didn't want to, when I only wanted to grab her and run away so we would never be apart.

In a perfect world, I would get my happy ending, but sometimes life, especially for me, would never be perfect. I might not get my happy ending, but watching Lilith laugh and talk with the others, I knew she would finally get hers. Maybe it just wouldn't be with me.

Maybe, I'd been defeated.

Chapter 20

Alec

THICK TENSION SWIRLED through the loud room, and my friends talked and laughed as if they couldn't feel it. No, they ignored it, which meant they ignored me.

I sulked in the corner, picking at a napkin I'd swiped from the table. I felt sick, and each chuckle I heard made my stomach lurch even more. I wanted, no needed, to run from the room and never look back at any of them. I couldn't, though. Instead, I listened as CG, Jase, or even Jaxson asked question after question to Lilith. She answered each with an energy I hadn't seen from her in years.

I was proud of her for what she'd accomplished. She hadn't been telling me her stories, but I heard them nonetheless. I could admit she'd put in the work to heal, but I noticed something else too. She almost seemed to ignore all the events that brought her to the point of needing to enter a facility. The reason she had to get treated. Nobody mentioned it, and she sure didn't either. She may want to forget about it, act like it never happened, but she needed to talk about it. Accept it. Admit it happened. Or she'd never really recover.

The day she left for treatment, and everything that came before, weren't the only things she'd forgotten. Anytime anyone mentioned something that happened in the past, a memory we all shared; she steered the conversation in a different direction.

My heart ached to sit next to her, hold her hand, and give her one of my best smiles. I wanted to be able to join the conversation now, to laugh with them and listen to all she went through while she was away. To share with Lilith how much we'd all missed her, especially me. I knew they weren't leaving me out on purpose; they just knew how hard it would be for me to be a part of it right now.

Markus was like a leech and hadn't left her side all evening. Every move she made, he made with her. They finished each other's sentences, got each other things to eat, and all the other bull that goes along with that. I fought the anger hard, but it still threatened to burst out of my chest. I kept my eyes cast down after a while, so I didn't have to see them anymore. I couldn't do it much longer. I wanted to give up, not completely, but almost.

"She's happy, you know," a deep voice said from beside me.

I squeezed the napkin when the leech's voice wrapped around me. Apparently, he could remove himself from Lilith's side. Who knew? I didn't respond. I owed him nothing. I'd stayed here, listened to their conversations. I'd tried. That was all I owed anyone. I might have been defeated in the battle for Lilith's heart, and I could accept that, but it didn't mean I still wasn't angry.

"She made so much progress with her time in the treatment

center, she doesn't need to relapse." Markus's accusatory tone made me glance up. He stared down at me, but I met his eyes and didn't flinch.

After several seconds with neither of us backing down, I asked, "What's that supposed to mean?"

"Don't mess up her happiness just because you didn't get what you wanted," he said, his tone cutting through my skin.

"Oh, and what is it that you think I want?" I sat up straighter.

"None of us are stupid, Alec. You obviously thought she'd be coming home and running right back to you." He turned to face me fully. "And you're not bothering to hide your feelings about the situation. Not since we walked in."

"Well...how the fuck do you expect me to feel? When she left, you weren't part of the equation," I couldn't keep my voice from rising.

"That no longer matters. I'm part of it now, and that's not going to change anytime soon. Don't be selfish."

My eyes widened at his words, and it took every bit of strength I had not to stand straight up and yell right in his face. Instead, I slowly made my way to my feet, looking down at his smaller figure.

"Selfish? Me, really? How in the hell am I the selfish one in all of this?"

"None of this would have happened if it weren't for you."

He lowered his voice but that made the words bite into me. A whimper almost escaped, but somehow, I held it back. I took a few staggering steps behind me as if I'd been slapped. My eyes scanned the room. Nobody had noticed us talking. When my gaze fell back to him, he smiled crookedly.

"I didn't do this. Lilith, she chose to do what she did—"

He put his palm in the air. "Yeah, because of you. Everything was fine until you got in her damn head." He shook his head, stepped a tad closer to me and lowered his voice even more. "Lilith and I are the ones who are supposed to be together, not you, not ever, so get used to it."

I stopped the chuckle from escaping, but it still echoed in my head. I leaned in closer, making sure he could hear me and said what I'd been wanting to say for a while. "Just remember, Markus, you were paid to be her boyfriend, hired for her affection. I received it because she gave it to me freely. That kind of makes you a male prostitute, doesn't it?" I smirked.

His shoulders shook and his chest deflated, but he smirked right back at me in the end. "It might have started like that, but now, I'm the one she's going to marry."

The entire room froze. I couldn't move anything but my mouth, and it gaped open so wide, a spider could weave a web in it.

Marry.

No way. No how. He didn't mean it. He had to be mistaken. Marriage came when two people who loved each other wanted to spend the rest of their lives together. Lilith couldn't want that with him. Could she?

I couldn't get out of my own head. An eerie silence wrapped

around me. I heard people calling my name, but it sounded distant. My eyes moved to Lilith, who touched her chin to her chest, but kept my gaze on her. I couldn't take my eyes off her if I wanted to. My heart ran a marathon in my chest, trying to get to the finish line before anyone else.

Markus had to be lying, and I'd be a fool to believe him, to let his words have such an effect on me. My eyes flitted over Jase, CG, and Jaxson and fell back to Lilith. Concerned looks stared back at me. I couldn't reassure them. Not right now, when I couldn't even move, let alone speak.

"Alec? What's wrong?" Lilith voiced her concern out loud.

My chest rose and fell, but my breaths were so uneven it didn't feel like I had gotten any oxygen to my brain.

"M-Married...you're getting—" I swallowed. Hard. "*Married?*" The words tumbled from my lips, and I stared at her, begging and pleading with my eyes for her to contradict them.

Eyes widened all around her, the band turning to her with raised brows. None of that worried or bothered me, but when Lilith took a deep breath and her shoulders relaxed as every bit of uneasiness fell from her face—that bothered me. It didn't look like the thought of marriage terrified her at all. She smiled and met Markus' gaze, pressing her lips together.

"You told him?" She scurried to his side and he wrapped an arm around her waist.

"Sorry, Lil, I let it slip on accident," He grinned down at her.

The tape holding my heart together ripped. Hearing the

confirmation from her lips...nothing could take that pain from me. Nothing could heal the damage those words inflicted. I'd lost the battle with no chance of fighting back.

Lilith and Markus were getting married.

Chapter 21

Alec

"LILITH? ANSWER ME... please," I whispered, trembling in anticipation of her response.

She lifted her gaze from Markus and looked at each one of our shocked faces. "It's true. Although I wanted to be the first to tell you," she chuckled, looking at the giggling maniac beside her. "We're engaged to be married."

Her words, spoken with such pride and happiness, slapped me right in the face. I took a long stride away from her but didn't take my eyes from her. She gaped, obviously waiting for her congratulations, but nobody could do anything but stare at her in stunned silence.

Everyone knew what had happened between Lilith and me that last day in the hospital. We'd shared our love and made promises. It took everything in me to hold back and not shout everything back at her.

"W-Why?" I choked out.

The smile slipped from her face as lines wrinkled her forehead. "What do you mean why?" She paused. "We love each other, Alec. We've been together for over two years. Obviously, it was only a matter of time before it would happen."

I stood there, gawking, in a complete daze. I didn't know what was going on. I didn't understand. It seemed like we'd made no progress at all and we'd reverted to when Markus was her fake boyfriend. Like she'd forgotten everything that came after. How had this happened? I hadn't been ready for it. No way, in a million years, had I ever thought any of this would happen when she returned. In fact, it was the absolute last thing I'd have ever imagined.

"But what about me...us?" I squeezed the words out.

"Alec, dude, come on. I thought you understood that was a long time ago?" she smiled.

I cringed when she said 'dude'. I'd entered the friend zone. "Over? We talked about this in the hospital before you left. Have you forgotten everything?" I raised my voice.

Jaxson made his way over to me, placing a hand on my shoulder. "Breathe, Alec."

My shoulders rose and fell quickly with each deep breath I took. CG and Jase had taken their places next to each other off to the side as they watched everything. My eyes though, stayed on the couple in front of me, the couple that shouldn't be together.

"Alec, I remember *everything*, okay?" Lilith's voice turned harder than her cheerful tone earlier. "I went through hell, and I finally feel like I'm in a good place, and that place includes Markus."

"You weren't even really together before!" I screamed, and Jaxson flinched beside me.

"You don't know everything, Alec, so stop acting like you do!" Lilith yelled back at me as Markus pulled her to his side. "Whatever you think was real or not back then doesn't matter because what's real is now. I love him and want to spend the rest of my life with him. If you can't accept that, you were never really my *friend* at all," she spat.

I stared her dead in the eyes. "Maybe that's because I was never *just* your friend, Lil. I was your boyfriend," I said to her.

A flicker of emotion passed over her face, but she shook her head and shrugged. "That's in the past, Alec, and this—" she gestured between herself and the silent guy beside her. "This is my future. You can either accept it or not."

At that moment, our eyes locked and never left or faltered to the others. The room became deathly silent, and no one dared say a word. I felt Jaxson's hand on my back; CG and Jase remained off to the side, attached to each other.

The room darkened around me, and it was almost as if the darkness seeped into my veins. The light and happiness I once felt vanished, replaced by a cold darkness.

A low chuckle escaped my lips as I lowered my gaze and shook my head. My feet moved forward of their own accord, and I brushed past Lilith, bumping into her shoulder as I said, loud enough for the whole room to hear, "I choose to not." With those final words, I slammed the door behind me.

I had gone home later that night and refused to answer the phone or talk to anyone. I needed a night to get my thoughts sorted and figure out what I wanted. After hours of thinking and tugging at my hair, I came to one conclusion: Lilith could no longer be a part of my personal life.

***

I have mentioned before, whoever came up with the saying "time can heal all things" was full of crap. Time didn't heal anything; it only made everything worse. Made everything sitting inside boil to the surface, causing an eruption of bitterness and hate. Time aged pain and hurt over time, but unlike a fine wine getting better with age, pain got worse. How in the hell could people tell me time would heal my broken heart? I'd given it plenty of time, and no healing had taken place.

I had given it six months' worth of my damn time to be exact. Six extra months to work through an even deeper pain than I had imagined, everything sitting on my chest like concrete, getting heavier every day. There were days my bones felt like they were being crushed by the weight of it all, snapping like twigs thrown to the ground.

In the beginning, I thought it would get easier. Hell, I thought it would get better, but it never did. I had. I'd listened to the tale of how two people apparently fell in love and got engaged. I listened to how they wanted a late summer wedding at the lake house that the band had purchased a few summers ago. And hearing it all made every bit of my sanity float away.

Six months of hearing about flower arrangements, tuxedos,

bridesmaid dresses, and guest lists. No one could stop talking about Markus this and Lilith that and it made my head spin, but the worst part—the part that stung more than anything—was they didn't include me in a single conversation about the wedding.

Jase, CG, and Jaxson kept me informed, but they didn't talk about it much. Hearing it from my place on the sidelines killed me. I had to act as if I'd disappeared from the face of the earth so Lilith could hold on to her happiness. And so, it had been six months since I'd decided to cut Lilith from my life.

I couldn't take her out of my working life since we were in a band, but that was all our relationship became. A business relationship, nothing more. She never tried to make it any more than that, and neither did I. The others tried for a while but eventually gave up. It would never happen, and they finally understood.

The band had started to work together more since Lilith's treatment, but it was a slow process. She still had doctor and therapy appointments but was doing well. So well, in fact, that she and Markus had been able to plan their upcoming wedding that seemed to involve everyone.

Everyone had been helping them to make their special day brilliant. Everyone except me. I showed up to work, and afterward, I went home to my apartment. Alone. Sometimes Jaxson, CG, or Jase would come over, but there was an unspoken rule that Lilith was not invited.

I thought I would feel better once I cut Lilith out of my life. In some ways, it helped. I didn't have to see *his* smiling face beside her. But, it hurt too. I'd lost a great friend.

I tried to convince myself we hadn't been on the best terms before this all happened anyway but never had it been as bad as it was now. We didn't interact much during our working hours. It had come to the point we hardly acknowledged one another's existence. Part of me didn't care, the other part always would.

Sundays were the worst. The loneliest. If we weren't working, the others went out, and I sat alone in my house. Once in a while, I'd take a drive to see my parents. But not often, it took too much effort to get dressed.

Today, the gray skies and drizzle kept me inside. It didn't matter. The dreary day matched my mood. Instead, I'd sat on my sofa and stared out the window, watching the rain for the past three hours.

My mind wouldn't steer clear of the upcoming wedding. I didn't know the exact date. But I knew it had to be coming up fast. The other members of the band were part of the wedding party. I didn't even know if I'd been invited or not. I'd made up my mind, even if I were, I wouldn't step foot anywhere near the ceremony. To me, that would be accepting their relationship and marriage, and I would never do that. I wouldn't accept something built on lies and never meant to be real. I still couldn't wrap my mind around why Lilith chose him. Why, out of every person in the world besides me, she chose to be with *him*. It made no sense. I wasn't sure it ever would.

My thoughts were suddenly interrupted by a knock on the door. With a sigh, I heaved myself up and made my way through the foyer to open the door. Jaxson stood there with a small frown on his face but fought a smile as he pulled me in for a big hug.

"Hey man, how're you doing?" he asked me as he followed me

inside.

I shut the door and led him into the living room, offering him a seat on the couch before I slouched into my previous position. "Eh, I'm okay I suppose. You?" I asked him.

He shrugged. "Same old same old, I guess." He ran a hand through his hair. "Look, Alec, I was asked to come by and drop something off for you. As much as I *don't* want to do this because I know it's just going to piss you off... I promised." He avoided eye contact.

"Okay, what is it?" I asked, confused.

He sighed and sat up straighter before pulling out a square pale pink envelope. In my mind, I already knew what it was and, I swallowed thickly while staring at it.

"Here you go." He handed it to me.

It felt like a thousand pounds in my hands as I looked at my name delicately printed on the front it. Sweat formed on my forehead, and my hands shook a little bit.

Without thinking about what I was doing, my trembling fingers opened the envelope and pulled out a piece of cardstock paper. The elegant designs over the pretty pink paper stood out beautifully with the occasional flower printed here and there. The swirls melded together into a beautiful collage. The splashes of summer colors sprung up onto the paper, bringing it all together. It was nice to look at, but that didn't take away the words typed in the middle of it all.

Together with friends and family

Lilith Ashley Rose

And

Markus James Stewart

Request the honor of your presence at their wedding on

July 31st

The rest of the words blurred together as I remained stuck on one line in the invitation: July 31st. The wedding is in *one week*.

Chapter 22

Alec

"PLEASE TELL ME this is some kind of joke..." I stuttered to Jaxson. I'd felt like I couldn't breathe plenty of times before, but it didn't hold a candle to what I felt now. Every bit of air I pulled into my lungs was like a sharp-edged saw that punctured everything on the way back out. On top of the pain, it didn't feel like I'd gotten any oxygen and now my lungs might collapse from the struggle.

"Trust me, dude—I wish I could say it was," he sighed, running a hand through his dark hair. "This whole thing has been a nightmare. To be honest, I still don't believe it's happening."

The room fell silent, and I stared at Jaxson, rubbing my chin. All this time, I'd thought he'd been happy for Lilith and Markus, even excited to be a part of the wedding. I guess my own issues blinded me. I had once again fooled myself into thinking everyone was okay, but now, seeing Jax like this, maybe I'd been wrong.

Jaxson wore dark circles wrapped around his eyes. Had he been sleeping? I didn't know since I hadn't paid attention. Frown lines embedded around the corners of his mouth, making me wonder if he'd smiled recently. He looked more than worn out; he looked exhausted. I hadn't noticed. Even after everything Lilith had gone through, I'd have done the same thing again.

"I'm so sorry." I rubbed my forehead, and my hand covered my eyes before I dropped both arms to my side.

He lifted and angled his head toward me. "For what?"

"For not being here for you." I looked down at the invitation, which I still held in my hands. "All this time I've been so focused on being angry and bitter at the world…it made me forget I have three other friends, best friends, that I can rely on. And maybe, just maybe, they need me too."

"You know you could have *four* other best friends, right?" He touched his chin to his chest and peered at me.

I shook my head before he even finished his words. "I—I can't, Jaxson. It's too much…"

"I know, I know." He patted my knee gently. "But you're right. We do need you, Alec, and I know you can't see it, but this is all driving us crazy."

I furrowed my eyebrows together, gaping at him. "What do you mean?"

"Alec, they're driving us insane! No one wants this wedding to happen—except those two. Everyone is going through the motions and doing their jobs because we want to make Lilith happy, but I just—" He rushed through his speech before stopping abruptly and staring down at my dark cherry wood floors.

"You just what?" I asked, holding my breath.

"I don't think she'll ever really be happy without you, Alec," his tone held sincerity.

I snorted at him. "She's been fine for the past six months, Jaxson. She's made it clear she doesn't need me anymore."

He slammed his hand against the coffee table. "But that's just it. Once again, you don't have a clue. When are you going to open your fucking eyes?" his yells bounced off the walls, slamming into me.

"Hey, I've been dealing with a lot of crap, if you haven't noticed." I countered.

"Yeah, yeah, yeah. Spare me from hearing your sob story again. Maybe if you weren't so damn focused on you and your feelings, if you just took a minute to look at the things around you, maybe then you'd realize Jase, CG, and I need you. So does Lilith," he lowered his voice.

"She doesn't need me because she has him," I screamed, standing up and throwing the invitation down on his lap. "If she needed me, I wouldn't be looking at this crap right now, or it would have my name on there instead of his." Tears pricked my eyes, and a lump swam in the back of my throat.

"Alec, your name should be the one on this and hell, one day when it is, please make it a lot less girly looking,"

I smirked as he stood, making strong eye contact with me.

"Alec, they were never in love. Even now, it's written all over Lil's face. The way she acts with him? It's just like before. Like it's all written out, a love script. It's not natural, and whether you want to see it or not, her eyes light up the second you walk into a room. She gravitates toward you, but she fights it. Hard. Probably because of that thick brick wall you've built around yourself. She knows you won't let her back in, but you need to, and you need to do it quick."

"Jax I—"

"No, Alec. You have to put an end to this charade and take back what's yours." He crossed his arms over his chest.

"But it's—" I stopped and sighed, "She's not mine anymore. She chose him." I stared at my feet.

He sighed softly and stepped forward, wrapping his arms around me and patting my back in a tight man-hug. "Her mind may have chosen him, but her heart will always choose you."

The strings of my heart tugged at his words, and I felt the flicker of hope I thought had died light up again. My mind and heart were at war now, though. My heart screamed at me to fight for her, while my mind told me to stick with my decision and let her go.

"Alec, you have to fight for her. You both gave up the first time. Don't make the same mistake again." He stepped back and walked toward the door, dropping the invitation back onto the coffee table. Then he left.

Once again alone in the quiet of my apartment, my thoughts bombarded me. With shaky fingers, I reached forward to pick up the invitation and stared at it as if it held the answers I needed. After a few minutes, determination rose up inside of me. Jaxson had been right. She shouldn't be with him. She wasn't supposed to marry *him.* That was my place and no one else's. Even her name should never be listed beside his. He didn't deserve a spot beside her, and he certainly didn't deserve a place in her heart. I knew Lil better than anyone, and she reserved her heart for the people who meant the most to her, and I should be in there, and damn it if I wouldn't make sure I was again.

It was time to get my Lilith back for good.

Chapter 23

Alec

WITH A RENEWED mind and more hope than I had felt in a long time, the week went by faster than ever. People were flying in from all over the world to attend the wedding and weekend festivities. Everyone bustled about to get everything organized and ready for the big day, but I just sat waiting in my apartment.

I wasn't asked once throughout the week to help do anything, and although I preferred that, it was still a bit frustrating. I knew they wouldn't call, but I guess some part of me hoped they would. The entire week had been spent sitting alone in my apartment trying to decide how to turn my newfound change of heart into a plan of action. I had no leads and no fucking clue what to do now. Choosing to get her back was one thing, but now actually doing it terrified me.

The media and the fans expected me to attend the wedding. Everyone did, except for the ones in our inner circle. I wouldn't be there, and if I had my way, nobody would. No, if I had my way, there wouldn't be a wedding. Now, I needed a plan to convince her to stop the wedding. Easy, right?

The week had come and gone, and now it was Friday, exactly one day before the wedding. The ceremony would take place twenty-four hours from now, and while the groom's side of the wedding party had opted to stay at home, relaxing on a quiet evening, the bandmates were at a party. Jaxson had sent me a text, begging me to come. I wanted to, but with my ass implanted into the couch cushions, it made it almost impossible to move.

Lilith wanted a bachelorette party, one last "hoorah". She didn't have many friends outside of the band, so if I didn't go, it would look really bad on my part. But if I did go...the debate in my head dragged on and on. If I went, she might think I'd accepted her upcoming nuptials, and I certainly had *not.* But if I didn't go, the media would surely throw it in my face. There were pros, and there were cons.

In the end, the pros won out. One in particular. I had a feeling if I went it could be the game changer I needed. So, without any more hesitation, I flew upstairs to my room to change and get ready. Tonight, I'd be heading to a club with my best friends and my ex to celebrate her upcoming wedding. The one that was never going to happen. Not if I could help it.

When I arrived and walked through the entrance, I squinted against the neon lights and bright-colored strobes piercing the darkness. I had to weave through a sea of people almost piled on top of each other. Some were dancing, and some were drinking. Some were doing both and looking the fool. Music blared, and the floors shook from the beat. The heat made sweat drip down the back of my neck. I'd picked the wrong night to wear a long-sleeved shirt.

As I got closer to where I thought my friends might be, my stomach did a little flip followed by a flop and a drop, like a ride at an amusement park. I hadn't spoken to Lilith outside of working terms in over six months, and tonight I planned to tell her everything. I pictured her rejection slapping me in the face. I could even imagine her asking me to leave. It scared me to death, but I had to take a risk or lose her forever. If I didn't chance it, I'd never know, and she'd end up married to an idiot for the rest of her life. I had to try to fight. At least a little.

"Alec?" someone yelled from behind me.

I turned to find CG, her eyes glazed and a lopsided smile plastered on her face. She must be drunk already. She leaped at me, and I caught her in a hug.

"What the heck are you doing here?" She screamed into my ear. "Not that I'm not happy to see you, because I am, it's just I didn't expect you here, and we haven't talked in a while and hey, did you cut your hair?" She tilted her head to the side.

I chuckled. "A little much to drink so early in the night, CG?"

She shrugged. "Can't help it with all the senior citizens I brought here with me. They've barely talked all night," She groaned.

"The guys?" I cupped my ear thinking maybe I'd be able to hear her response.

She gave a nod and almost fell forward, but quickly righted herself. "Yeah, I had to lie and tell them I had to use the little girl's room just to get away. As loud as it is in this club, it's deathly silent over there." She shook her head and led me over to the bar. "Let's get you a drink, or else I'm kicking your ass right back out the door." She grinned and yelled at the bartender to grab me a beer.

I smiled as CG talked to the bartender, moving her hands through the air. Her words came out slurred and hard to understand. CG was always happy, but when drunk, it kicked the happiness up a notch. She also became a little grabby. Before, it was always directed at Jase. I slapped my forehead with my palm. I never noticed anything with those two, but even back then, I must have been blind not to see it.

CG turned to me. "So then, I was like, 'I really don't care about the flower arrangements', and Lilith flipped on me. But I mean, come on, who the hell cares if you have lilies or roses. It was all, 'which do you think Markus would prefer?'" She stuck a finger down in her throat like she wanted to make herself throw up and handed me my beer.

"C—" I went to stop her from talking about the wedding.

She ignored me, acting as if I hadn't started speaking at all. She grabbed my arm, leading me away from the bar. "So then, I told her if she was so concerned about what *he* wanted, she should just have her overcontrolling fiancé doing this because he's done everything else, and now she hasn't talked to me in like two weeks."

"Wait. CG, you actually said that to her?" I gaped at her.

"Well, hell, Alec. She was concerned about how many goddamn petals each flower had on it because Markus told her if it was an odd number it meant bad luck." She threw her hands up in the air but

198

didn't stop walking.

I shook my head, grinning so big my cheeks hurt. "I love drunk CG," I said to myself as I followed her, squeezing through a horde of dancing people.

We went up a set of stairs in the back corner of the building and rested on a raised platform overlooking the dance floor. It was less crowded up here and easier to see the entire room. I saw CG take a deep breath before she turned a corner and said something I couldn't hear over the music. I bit my lip and rounded the corner, pausing to look at the band. Jase's mouth parted when he saw me, but Jaxson only smirked.

CG, who stood blocking me, sidestepped so Lilith, who sat in the middle of a couch, met my gaze. Her eyes widened, and she swallowed hard. She didn't blink once, at least not that I could see.

She looked just as beautiful now as the day I met her. I took in her blue eyes, a color I'd never seen until hers, and her light blonde hair that darkened in the winter and lightened in the summer. Her sun-kissed skin, so soft I'd never forget it, even though I hadn't touched it in so long. To me, she didn't have a single imperfection. From the top of her head to her plump red lips to her huge feet. It was all flawless.

I'd dreamed of being with her again, of learning every curve of her body again. I wanted to kiss her forehead and dip down to get the tip of her nose and end with her lips. I needed to trace the lines of her body, worship her like the goddess she was. I dreamed of loving her, giving her every bit of passion I could and desiring everything about her.

"Alec?" her soft voice questioned.

I bit my lip to hide the smile threatening to explode on my face. "H-Hey, Lil."

"Why are you here?" She rubbed the back of her neck.

"Honestly?" I inched forward, and she nodded, leaning back to stare up at my tall form. "I'm not really sure...just felt like I should be."

"But I thought you didn't *approve*?" She pressed her lips together.

"I don't, but I still wanted to be here—for you." I didn't take my eyes off her.

"Alright guys, let's go get us a round of drinks, yeah?" Jaxson interrupted, standing up and dragging a clingy CG and Jase with him.

The tension doubled as soon as we were alone. I stayed put, unable to move, even if I wanted to, until Lilith patted the couch next to her. I slid into it, holding her gaze.

Several quiet seconds passed before I finally asked, "Why are you doing this?"

She sighed and gave a sarcastic laugh. Her tone sounded tired.

"Okay, fine, then, but I don't understand."

She rolled her eyes. "What more is there to understand? I love him, Alec, and I want to be with him." She left no room for argument, the confidence in her tone making it seem like her decision was the most obvious thing in the world.

"How can you say you love him, Lil? Your so-called relationship was based on lies. Oh, and acting. Can't forget that." I clenched my

200

jaw, trying to hold the anger at bay.

She rolled her hands into tight fists, stood, and glared at me. "You don't know anything, Alec! Forget everything I said before I left. Focus on what's happening tomorrow. *I'm getting married.* Not because I have to, but because I want to," her voice boomed over the loud music.

I tapped a finger against my chin, thinking before I spoke again. "Okay, fine but can I ask you one question?"

"Didn't you already do that?" she sighed.

"Just one more. Please?"

She paced back and forth but finally nodded. I took a deep breath.

"Are *you* happy?"

A look passed over her face, one I couldn't describe. Her stiff shoulders drooped and her mouth gaped open. She breathed deeply through her nose, not responding for a few minutes. I'd started to think she would never answer, or if she did, she would lie.

"Yes." No emotion passed over her, and there wasn't a bit of inflection in her voice. She spoke stiffly as if talking about the weather.

I nodded. "Okay. You're happy. I'll respect that but..."

"*But what*, Alec?" she asked, exasperated.

I crossed my leg over my knee and leaned back, taking a sip of my beer. "You have an opportunity here. One last night of fun. One last night of being single. That means no regrets."

"What the hell does that me—"

I never gave her the chance to finish. Instead, I shot up, dropping my beer to the floor. I took both cheeks in my hands and crashed my lips against hers. I felt her tense beneath me and thought she might push me away, but I moved my lips against hers, putting every bit of passion into the kiss. I kissed her with every fiber of need floating through me, every bit of love that had never left me. I kissed her like I would if it was our last kiss, and I didn't give up.

With persistence came results. Lilith wrapped her arms around my neck and kissed me right back, matching my fire with her own. I didn't know where the others were and I didn't care. If thoughts rolled into my mind, I might lose out on this chance and I couldn't let that happen.

I lifted her up, my lips never leaving hers, and proceeded to guide her out the back and down an all too familiar path. It took me ten minutes to get to where I was going, three blocks north and two floors up. I sat Lilith down for just one moment to pull the keys out of my jeans pocket.

My fingers fumbled with the keys as I pressed Lilith against the door, never letting my lips leave hers. Her small hands gripped the front of my shirt, keeping me held against her. My one free hand stayed glued to her hip, pressing both of us firmly against each other.

"Alec, I swear to God if you don't open the door—"

I smirked against her lips as the door finally fell open, and we stumbled inside. She didn't waste a moment of her last night of freedom, slamming me against the wall in my foyer. She kicked the door shut with her foot and kissed me so deeply my head spun, but who needed to breathe at a time like this?

Lilith's hands ran up the length of my chest and back down again. My hands pinched her waist as I all but shoved us down the hallway. Our lips never parted, and it became even more heated with each step we took.

My mind couldn't process how I'd ended up in my room with Lilith pressed under me on my bed. I couldn't think of anyone else. Her smell. Her taste. It consumed me. When I'd hoped for this moment, this chance, I'd wanted it to be sweet. Loving. Soft. But the hungry look in Lilith's eyes told me it would be anything but.

Her hands reached down for the hem of my shirt, and I sat back on my knees as she lifted it up over my head. Her eyes roamed down the contours of my tattooed chest, her hands following right after them. Shivers sent goosebumps down my arms and legs. The feel of her hands, those hands and what they were doing to me, sent me into a crazed lust I never thought I'd feel again.

Chapter 24

Alec

I USED TO think happiness was just an illusion. Something people made up to tell an engaging story or to sell a good book. I never thought it existed for me, mainly because I usually got the opposite. While at one point in my life I'd truly been happy, it'd all stopped. Vanished like smoke in the wind. There'd not been a single trace left behind, and with it gone, a part of me had died. It had been so long since I'd been happy, I thought I'd live the rest of my life this way. Until now.

The bright sun shining through the curtains of my bedroom window made me stir. All my senses heightened in the early morning. Every damn chirp of a bird or soft snore beside me intensified like they sounded through a loudspeaker or something. A slight pain in my head made me wince. The ebbing behind my eyelids forced me to close them. But I didn't want to. I wanted to take it all in. Bask in my glory.

As my body woke up, warmth wrapped around me, and for the

first time in forever, I felt alive. Wholly alive.

Lilith's small body was tucked into my side, her arms wrapped around my middle. Her head covered my chest, and her breath fanned my stomach. Her light hair covered the top of my chest near my collar bone, and it tickled every time I took a breath or moved. Lilith's long, slender legs were entwined with my own, completing my sense of warmth and security. My body was bigger and more masculine, yet I was the one feeling safe and protected. A feeling I intended to treasure and keep sacred.

A slight stirring against my body made me crack my eyes open, but only a little. I instantly regretted it as light flooded the room, making me groan. I blinked several times until my eyes adjusted, and once I could see I looked down and the image took my breath away.

My mind played back everything from last night like I was watching a movie. From the ride from the club, to each drink, to the end. Every passionate kiss. Our bodies tangled together. The power of the moment couldn't be mistaken for some drunken and forgotten mistake.

Waking up next to Lilith had always been my favorite when it came to our earlier relationship. With her arms draped over me, I knew no danger would find me. In the same way, my arms supported her. My love, my adoration for her would never falter. She could hurt me, even break me, but I'd always be here, with open arms to invite her back in. I'd stand as a shield in front of her, die a thousand and one deaths, I'd take unimaginable pain if it meant the harm wouldn't touch her.

Waking up now, even though my head throbbed and my body ached, a calm washed over me. Maybe everything had changed last night. Maybe things would finally go my way. Maybe, after all these years, we'd get the chance to live out our happiness. With each other. I could feel it in my veins. It was finally our time.

My chest vibrated under a gruff voice speaking directly into it. My hand snaked into her hair, and I splayed my fingers through it, letting each strand fall between the spaces. She moved against me, and her chin dug into my chest as her eyes met mine. I'd prayed for this moment for so long. Had hardly allowed myself to hope for it. I couldn't take my gaze from her eyes, full of so much more life than a month ago. Her long lashes fluttered as her eyes drifted closed. I didn't stop playing with her hair.

"Alec?"

She broke the silence with my name on her lips, making even more warmth swirl through my chest. I smiled and mumbled back an inaudible response. I couldn't stop looking at her, memorizing every line, every feature of her beautiful face.

And then my stomach dropped, remembering what today was. Her wedding. I shouldn't be worried, should I? She'd been in my bed last night. Not his. In my arms. Not his. She wouldn't go through with it. Would she? With my whole world wrapped in my arms, I hoped not.

"I have a headache." Lilith sat up, rubbing her forehead.

I chuckled, but the laugh quickly turned to a groan as a throbbing pulsated through my head, too.

"You too?" she asked, and I could hear the smirk in her voice.

"Yeah," I mumbled back in a scratchy voice.

Her fingers danced patterns over my stomach, tracing lines or running circles over tiny moles. We let the silence of the morning wrap around us. It felt like old times. Nothing to worry about but love and us. Like it should be.

"Alec...did we...um..." Lilith asked, her fingers pausing.

A smile spreads across my face. "Yeah, babe, we did." I planted a kiss on the top of her head.

I'd imagined the comfortable silence we'd sat in. I imagined shock, but every scenario that played out in my head, they all ended in a happy Lilith. Not one time had I ever pictured her actual reaction. Nor did I plan for it.

"Crap!" She ripped herself away from me, sitting straight up. "Crap, crap, crap!" She gasped, jumping out of the bed, collecting her scattered clothing.

"Lilith?" The thin cotton sheet pooled around my waist as I shifted on the bed. "What's wrong babe?"

She wiggled to pull her pants on. "Alec, we had *sex*." She yanked her t-shirt over her head, then stopped moving and stared at me like she'd seen a ghost. Her skin even turned a shade whiter. I reached for my boxers, slipping them on as hopped to my feet in front of her.

"Yeah? I still don't understand what's wrong..."

"I'm getting married today." She spun around, searching for something. She dropped to her knees grabbing a shoe from under the bed, crawling under it to look for the other.

"You say that like you're still going to." I tilted my head.

She slid from under the bed, both shoes gripped in her hands. She rose to her feet and faced me, eyeballing me. I couldn't read her, not that I'd ever been able to.

She sighed heavily and sat in a chair in the corner, pulling her shoes on, then stood in front of me again. "Alec...I am still getting married today."

Her words slammed into my chest, knocking the wind from me. I stumbled back a few steps, the back of my knees smacking into the mattress. My mouth fell open, unable to respond, to even form a coherent thought. The places my heart had been sewn back together shredded, leaving a gaping wound. Every wall I'd built around me crumbled, leaving me more vulnerable than I'd ever been.

She could see the battle waging in front of her, the one for my soul, but she did nothing but stand there, staring at me, seeing right through me but not seeing anything at all.

"Alec, this—this should have never happened. You know, that, right?" the tone of her voice made it sound like she was talking to a kid.

"What—I—Lilith..." I couldn't get enough air. Couldn't find any words. I never thought this would happen. And because I hadn't expected it, it shattered me, my world. Everything.

"Come on, Alec. Don't make this harder than it needs to be, okay?" She sighed and reached over, picking up her phone from the bedside table. She checked it before slipping it into her pocket and standing up straighter than before.

"Lilith, I—"

"Look, Alec, I have to go get ready. The wedding starts in a few hours." She spoke like nothing had happened. Like nothing had changed. Like she'd spent a fun night with friends, rather than cheated on her soon to be husband.

"Lilith, no!" I grabbed her arm, pulling her against me. She stared at me with wide eyes. Tears slid down my cheeks faster than rain in a storm.

"No," I bellowed. "I won't let you leave me again. I won't!" My fingers dug into her arm, and I realized I needed to pull back, but I couldn't.

She shook her head. "Alec, this—you and I—will never work out. Come on. I thought you knew that." She wouldn't meet my eyes.

"But, why? W—we're perfect for each other. I—I love you!" Desperation filled my tone, but I didn't care.

"But I don't love you, Alec!" She jerked her arm from my grip. "Why can't you understand that? I love him. Not you. Not you!" She almost sounded like she was trying to make herself believe the words.

"Because I can see it in your eyes, dammit." I grasped a fistful of hair, flinging it as I dropped my hands hard to my sides. "If you loved him, you wouldn't look so miserable right now at the thought of going back to him. Everything started with you and me. How can you marry him? After what we did last night?"

"Last night meant nothing," her voice boomed, so shrill I worried

209

my windows would break. She shoved at my chest, and my back slammed against the wall.

I flinched, but didn't take my eyes from her. She gripped my shoulders, pulling me forward and smashing me into the wall again. A moan ripped from my throat, but I didn't fight back.

She continued. "We had too much to drink. It meant nothing."

She dug her nails into my shoulders before releasing me, running out the door. Her hurried footsteps down the stairs whispered through the emptiness she'd left me standing in.

When the front door slammed, I broke and whispered, "But you didn't drink..."

Chapter 25

Lilith

I HAD TRIED to keep my distance from him. Every instinct inside me screamed for me to run back into his arms, but I fought so hard against it. My body craved his. My skin itched to feel his touch. But I couldn't give in. Not because I didn't want to because, God, did I ever. But I couldn't let myself. My weakness had always been Alec. It felt like I'd been created just for him. Maybe I had been, in some ways, but I couldn't let myself go down that dangerous road. It wasn't a game I was willing to play.

Ever since I first met him, the magnetic pull had snapped into place until we gave in. Nothing could separate us or pull us apart. We became a package deal, always together, always one. But outside interference ripped up apart and stripped both of us of all the things that had drawn us together in the first place.

So, I had to leave him.

And I'd spent years in pain because of it. I'd spun lies and grew to hate myself. That hatred festered until I'd hit my breaking point. Of course, nobody had known a thing until I'd shared my story with the world. Maybe it had been the worst decision I'd ever made, but I didn't believe that. No, I believed everything happened for a reason. Although looking back, I should have handled it differently. I wouldn't put my family and my friends through any of it. I'd resented them for sending me away, but eventually, I'd realized I needed help. I'd learned to cope. I'd learned to trust myself. I'd learned how to live again, and I'd turned my life around for the better.

Everyone thought I'd made a quick recovery. Boy did I have them fooled. I'd always been a good actress, and this time was no exception. Some days, a sense of peace enveloped me, and I felt like I was moving in the right direction. But other times...the black hole grabbed me and dragged me down and down with no hope of ever finding my way out. Those days were the worst. I had to fight the most, the hardest, mainly because I didn't have anyone fighting beside me.

No one understood the decisions I'd made since returning. I got it, really, I did. Everything contradicted what I'd said on the internet that day. They probably thought I'd forgotten my words, but I hadn't. I never would. Everything I'd said had been the truth, and none of it had changed.

I love Alec, but I can't have him. Not now...*not ever*.

I walked into my place, swinging the door shut behind me. The phone in my living room rang and rang, but I ignored it as I stomped up the stairs and into my room, slamming the door shut and locking it. Clenching my fists, I marched into the bathroom and stripped my clothes off.

With the water turned on and warming, I stepped under the heavy stream and rested my head against the tiled wall. I squeezed my eyes shut, fighting the images that bombarded my mind. Every touch, every kiss, seared through my brain on replay. Ever since I left his apartment, pictures from last night flashed through my head, but they were all followed by the broken image of him, standing in his living room, watching me leave. I'd see the way he kissed me last night; then his sad eyes haunted me. And so it went, until anger at what I'd said to him, how I'd hurt him yet again, shook my body so hard I almost slipped in the shower.

I would never understand how Alec could believe the lies I spat at him, but he did. Every. Single. Time. He took everything I said to heart, treasuring it. It might be endearing, sure, but in some ways, it was the most frustrating thing in the world. For him to hold on to my words like he did...I shook my head because I counted on him doing exactly what he did. I took advantage of him. Again.

Nothing I said to Alec this morning would ever be true. At first, I didn't think he'd believe a single word. But when he did...it was the worst feeling I think I'd ever had. I might be branded suicidal, they might all think I need to be watched, but every last one of them put blinders on when it came to Alec. No one could see the fragile boy he was. Not one of them had seen the signs I had. He was frail, like a thin piece of glass that would break with the tiniest prick. He'd always been like that. A small, insecure boy who believed everything anyone told him. The smallest things, if given to him, could be turned into a huge problem. Some might see it as a fault, but I didn't. No, it was just another piece of him. A part I would do anything to protect.

Fooling the world had been easier than I'd thought. I came out of rehab a "new person". A girl who'd forgotten her past and everything she'd been through. A woman who'd found love with an old boyfriend, if I could even call him that. Everyone believed every word that left my mouth, especially when Markus proposed and I accepted.

The lies continued, but eventually, even my closest friends—my bandmates, believed I loved Markus. Even Alec, but I'd laid it on thick for him. He needed to believe it the most. I never wanted to hurt him. I wanted to protect him and his heart. After everything we'd been through, being with me would never be enough for him. He loved me, but I would never be what was best for him. Alec deserved someone good, someone kind, someone who wasn't broken. I could never be that for him, even if I wanted to with every fiber of my being.

"Lilith. Come on; the car will be here any minute!" my mom shouted, trying to push the door open.

Good thing I'd locked the door. I climbed out of the shower and wiped the fog from the mirror, then with my palms against the counter I leaned forward. I didn't look at myself but instead stared at my shaking hands. I didn't move for a while, but when I did, I donned my wedding gown. I didn't look in the mirror, I knew the dress was beautiful. Markus had great taste, I'd give him that.

With a deep breath, I walked to the door and rested my hand on the knob. My other hand reached for the lock, and after a few seconds, I unlocked it. "Coming..."

I turned before I left, looking around the room. Boxes littered the floor, all of Markus' things he'd already started to move in. My heart hammered in my chest, realizing everything about Alec in this room would have to be removed. I could never fully remove him from my life since we were in the band together, but Markus would never stand for pictures of him in our private space. Could I do that? Remove his memories from my life, my heart?

I couldn't believe I was going to marry him. To go through with it. I'd have to live with him the rest of my life. Have a family with him. Tears pricked my eyes. I'd always thought I'd be standing next to Alec in my white gown, staring into his eyes as we said our vows. I wiped at my cheeks and opened the door. None of those things mattered anymore. I'd made my choice, and I'd stick to it to save him from a miserable life at my side.

My mom stood just on the other side and smiled, with tears gleaming in her eyes, as I walked out. "You look beautiful, honey." She paused and held her arms out. "Sweetie, what's wrong?"

I walked into her offered embrace and reveled in the feel of her hand rubbing against my back. I rested my head next to hers as I held her to me in a tight embrace. "Just thinking..." I murmured.

"You know I love you, right?" She pulled back so she could meet my eyes.

I nodded in reply.

"I just want to make sure this is what you want, Lilith. Please don't make a mistake. Just be honest with yourself about what it is you *really* want."

I swallowed the lump in my throat. I'd been horrible to them all. Lying to them, hurting them...and it was the last thing I'd wanted to do. My family meant everything to me. I cared for them more than I did myself. When I hurt them, it was like a stab to my chest. But I couldn't back down now. I couldn't share this burden with them. Or anyone. It was mine and mine alone.

"I am, Mom. I love Ma—I love *him*. I am marrying him, aren't I?" I whispered.

I couldn't dare say his name and a declaration of love in the same sentence. Not to my mom, the woman I trusted more than anyone in the world.

She sighed, and a slur of words left her mouth, but none I could quite catch. Then she slowed down.

"I support whatever you choose to do, darling." She pulled back and held me at arm's length with a soft smile. "If you're happy."

If I'm happy.

Happiness would never exist for me.

***

Soft music filled the air, but it didn't drown out the birds chirping or the rushing river behind us. We were at the lake house we bought a few summers ago. A big beautiful log home sitting away from the city near a private lake for only us and our guests. Trees surrounded the property, along with a beautiful variety of flowers. It had always been my favorite place to come with the boys and CG, a place holding so many memories I kept close to my heart. Now all those memories would be tarnished by the event taking place today.

People slowly filed in, all chatting and smiling about the wedding. I had to force the scowl off my face as they laughed and congratulated me. I clenched my fists with my nails digging into my palms, but it was the only way I'd be able to keep my cool. I was miserable. My skin crawled, and my heart raced, pumping blood through my veins, which made my legs want to pump, to run away as fast as they'd carry me. But, I'd made up my mind, and I had to see this through. I'd marry Markus today and leave Alec alone.

"Lil?"

A soft voice made me turn to see Jase. Jaxson stood beside him, and CG jogged up behind them, holding her long, pale pink dress, so it didn't drag on the ground. I smiled, and this one reached my eyes. At least they were here. They'd support me, no matter what I did.

"Hey, guys." I gave them each a hug. When I stepped back, my eyes landed on CG's and Jase's hands, fingers woven together. A pang ripped through my heart, memories crashing to the surface, but I pushed them down. I couldn't dredge up the past and go through with this.

"You look stunning!" CG grabbed a corner of my veil, waving it through the air.

"Where did you run off to last night?" Jaxson asked, a corner of his mouth aimed at the sky. "You and Alec disappeared."

I froze, but shook it off, remembering the story I'd rehearsed. "He drove me home." I shrugged it off as it were nothing. I saw all their faces fall suddenly, and that confused me deeply.

"You went home?" Jase raised his brows, and I nodded. "What

about Alec?" he asked coolly.

"Don't know." I shrugged. "Haven't seen him since. We, uh, didn't exactly end the night on a high note." I let my eyes drift away and out toward the backyard where the guests were filling the seats.

"Oh... well, I'm sure he'll come," Jaxson said.

I snorted, shaking my head. "He won't come, Jaxson." I stared down at the dress Markus picked out for me.

I had never thought he would, and I hoped he didn't. I didn't think I could do this with him here. In fact, I know I couldn't.

"Well, I spo-" Jaxson started but was cut off when my mom rushed into the living room.

Mom grabbed my upper arm gently. "Boys, it's time." She smiled and looked at me. The smile didn't reach her eyes, but I didn't comment on that. I couldn't stand to see the look in her eyes, the hope I would put a stop to this mess.

"See you out there, Lil," Jase winked me.

My eyes swept over the guests and the property. They landed on the small stream behind us, and I couldn't help but smile at the fond memories hidden deep in my heart of Alec and me. We would spend hours trying to skip rocks together out there, only to conclude that neither of us could do it. We'd spend the nights lying on the bank and counting stars together. Simple moments I would count as blessings for the rest of my life.

The music loudened, bringing my attention back to the scene in front of me. My bridesmaids sauntered down the aisle, taking their places across from the guys. Everyone rose from their seats, turning toward the back, where I stood. It was time.

My breath caught in my throat as I saw Markus at the end of the aisle standing next to two of my best friends. My long white gown flowed behind me as I prayed not to fall in my three-inch heels. I went for simple and elegant even though I could tell Markus wanted me to dress more with a wow factor, but I got my wish.

Walking down the aisle with my dad took forever. He kept squeezing my arm in reassurance, and the further down we walked the faster the time went by. Before I knew it, I stood in front of Markus. I forced a smile toward the minister as he looked from one of us to the other.

"Who gives this woman to be married to this man?" he asked.

"Her mother and I do." My father smiled as he pressed a soft kiss to my cheek before placing my hand in Markus's.

Every bit of nervous energy I'd had doubled. Markus pulled me around to stand in front of him. I shot my best fake smile at him— well, the best I could manage. I tried to remind myself why I was doing this, why I was pretending to love him. I knew my hands were shaking, and my palms were dripping sweat into his, but I couldn't stop it. A sick feeling fell deep into the pit of my stomach.

"We are gathered here today to bring this man and this woman together in marriage," the priest began.

Sweat trickled down the back of my neck, and I forced myself not to look away from Markus as the priest continued.

"If anyone feels they shouldn't be married, speak now or forever hold your peace," deafening silence followed, not counting my galloping heartbeat.

Relief flashed across Markus's face when no one spoke out. The silence droned on for longer than necessary until murmurs and whispers clattered through the air. I narrowed my eyes at the minister, then at Markus, not sure what was happening. The whispers turned to loud conversations, and I turned, my dry throat making it hard to swallow.

There, walking down the small hill behind the guests and looking straight at me was the one person I had hoped wouldn't show. Alec.

"I have something to say about this union. It shouldn't be happening since Lilith and I had sex last night."

Chapter 26

Alec

NO GOING BACK now. I hadn't planned on saying anything, but when I laid eyes on Lilith, her long white gown shimmering in the sunlight, the words tumbled out faster than I could stop them. Gasps came from every direction around me, but I ignored them all and marched down the aisle, not taking my eyes off of Lilith. I could see the other boys fighting their smiles, and their gleeful looks only fueled my passion even more.

After Lilith left this morning, I had laid there against the wall for hours. I sobbed and banged my head against the wall, wanting to hurt myself, to make myself feel something. Anything. I couldn't catch my breath, and my heart leaped in my chest. Even with all of that going on, I couldn't get her last words out of my head.

"It was nothing more than an act of too much to drink..."

She'd left before I told her she hadn't drunk a drop. When I arrived at the club, she was just sitting there, no drink in hand. None on the table in front of her. None in her lap. She had complete control of herself, unlike CG. Plus, I'd kissed her, and she didn't taste like alcohol. She'd been completely sober, which meant she'd slept with me of her own free will.

The weight on my chest had crushed me as I tried to grasp what she was saying. It hadn't been a drunken mistake. No, she'd been in complete control of herself, could have stopped us at any moment. But she hadn't. She didn't pull away when I kissed her the first time, and she didn't when things got even more heated.

Sitting against my wall, it hit me like a freight train. If she hadn't drunk anything, she knew what she was doing; she knew the weight it would have on me. She wanted it, never even tried to push me away. She needed it as much as I did. Which meant she needed me, as much as I needed her. I could see it in her damn eyes the entire time we were together. There was no doubt or insecurity; it was all pure passion mixed with love. Everything had fallen into place until we woke up this morning.

I laid there for hours, doubt and self-loathing dragging me down until I figured it out. Newfound courage and a wave of expectancy rushed through me, and I realized I was so damn tired of being alone. I was tired of letting everything fall through the cracks. I didn't want to be the person that went along with everything because I didn't want to fight for what I wanted.

Lilith was *mine.* Nothing would change that. Not even a fake marriage. Last night, I envisioned smiling for the rest of my life at her side. That was the way it would have to be. I was done letting everyone else get what they wanted while I hid in the corner.

That was what led me here, walking down the aisle in front of everyone as I begged Lilith not to make this mistake.

"Alec? What are you doing here?" She rubbed her throat, her voice raspy. She didn't look at me, but at everyone else instead.

I didn't look away. "I came here to stop you from making a huge mistake."

"Alec, don't do this..." she begged.

I stopped and pressed my lips together. "No, Lilith. I won't let *you* do this. I've sat by too long and let you call the shots on everything, and I'm done. I'm so fucking done." I started toward her again.

Markus huffed and snapped around, his hands on his hips. "Can't you talk to her later, Alec? We're sort of in the middle of something."

"What are you talking about?" Lilith asked, ignoring her fiancé.

I let out a shallow sigh, shaking at the thought of what I was about to stay. But I didn't let the nerves stop me. "I let you walk away the first time. I didn't know what was going on behind closed doors, but I didn't fight for you. It hurt you, and I get that now." I shuffled closer, until I stood close, but not too close. "You had to leave me, and it killed you, but it hurt you more that I let you do it. I didn't put up a fight. I didn't argue with you or even slap you across the face. I didn't call you on the biggest mistake you've ever made in your life, and I—I regret that so much." I paused, taking a deep breath. I had to finish. Only a little more and it would all be out in the open. "I regret letting you walk out that day. It still haunts me now. It killed every bit of confidence I had, Lil. It destroyed me, to the point I don't even know how to think around you anymore. I'll tell you this, though: I love you. So much more than I ever thought possible, more than I did back then. This isn't a passing fancy. I won't change my mind. I need you, I want you, and I know you feel the same." I panted as if I'd been running a long-distance race. Sweat dripped down my forehead, but I didn't look away.

I watched every possible emotion flicker on her face. Her eyes met mine, shining as if she'd been clinging to every word I said like a prayer. Her teeth sunk into her bottom lip as she looked down at her shoes, sighing.

"Alec, we—you and I—we just can't," she said, so quiet I could hardly hear her.

"Why? Give me a damn good reason why," I said, my voice harsh even to my ears.

"Because you *think* you love me when you *don't*," she said, a little louder this time,

My confidence faltered, but only a little bit. I pressed on. "How could you say that?"

"It wasn't just the first time when I left you didn't fight for me, Alec!" she yelled, no doubt capturing everyone's attention now. "What about when I went away to treatment, huh? What about then?"

"Lilith, what are you talking about?" I said, my brows scrunching closer together.

"I never heard from you! You let me leave the hospital that day thinking everything would be perfect when I came back. I went away thinking you would be here waiting for me when I got back, but I leave for six months, and you just wipe me off your radar? How can you say you love me when you couldn't even be there for me when I needed you the most?" She clenched her hand and punched at the air in front of her.

My mouth dropped to the floor. She'd thought I left her? But, she'd left me...hadn't she? "Lilith, I—"

"No, Alec, don't even try to figure your way out of this one, okay? I don't need your excuses anymore. You gave up the fight a long time ago, and you weren't there when I needed you, but you know who was?" She angled her head. "He was. Markus helped me through it all. He saw me at my darkest hour and still never left my side. That is what love is, unconditional love." Her chest rose and fell rapidly.

My mind whirled. I never heard from her because she'd never heard from me. "But Lil, I didn't leave you. I sent letters, emails, everything..." A lump formed in my throat and tears lodged behind my eyes as I looked at her.

Her narrowed eyes told me there was no way she'd believe me.

"Please believe me."

She shook her head. "You need to leave, Alec...get over it. Get over me, *please.*" She turned back to Markus.

I stared at her, tears threatening to spill, but I sucked them in. Jaxson moved toward me, but I held up a hand to stop him. "I've let you walk out on me plenty of times. Please don't make me walk out of here alone, Lil," I pleaded.

She didn't face me. She didn't say another word. My shoulders slumped, and my feet dug into the grass below me. I tried to make her see. I tried to get her back. I fought this time, but she didn't want

225

to hear it. Maybe I'd been wrong. Maybe she didn't need me. Maybe she would never be able to forgive me for not putting up a fight the first time. Either way, I'd failed, and I felt defeated.

With my head down, I turned around and started walking back up the aisle, leaving my heart trampled and in pieces behind me.

"He's telling the truth," Markus's voice broke through the dead silence.

I froze, peering at them.

Lilith stared at him, those little lines all over her forehead. "What?"

"Alec. He's telling you the truth. He did send letters." He looked down at his shoes, suddenly interested in brushing off the nonexistent lint on his pants.

"You couldn't possibly know that," Lilith scoffed, and she looked up at him with tears in her own eyes.

"I do...because I have them." Everyone's eyes widened, and gasps could be heard from all directions at his confession, but their surprise couldn't rival mine and Lilith's. I stayed planted in my spot as I watched Markus try to explain.

"Despite what you may think, Alec, I do love Lilith. I always have. She's a great person with a beautiful soul, but I've always felt threatened. I know our relationship started as a business transaction, but I wanted to make it work...so much." He bit his lip and turned to look at Lilith.

"Mar—Markus. What are you saying?" she questioned.

"I'm saying I've done everything in my power to try and keep you two apart. I wanted you, Lilith. All of you. I could see that your heart belonged to him, but I thought maybe I could make you see how good we could be together, but now...I've made a horrible mistake."

"I still don't understand," Lilith said.

"Damn it, Lilith. When you went into the treatment center, I was still on your medical files as a person of contact. You were in the hospital, and no one had thought to change it. I called and spoke with your doctor about you and told him how I thought it was best if you only received mail, or anything, from certain people in your life. He thought it was understandable so you wouldn't be set back by those who triggered things in the first place. So I—I had Alec's letters taken out of your mail."

I stood there, hearing everything but in no way able to comprehend any of it. He'd been the reason she never heard from me and thought I had left her, given up on her. He had kept us apart and caused us to fall through the cracks. All so he could try to save a relationship that never existed in the first place.

"You lied to me?" she asked him, her voice cracking.

I watched her slowly start to break.

"I'm so sorry. I guess I hoped what you felt for him wasn't as deep as you thought, but I was wrong. So, so wrong. You both deserve to be together."

Lilith's eyes swept over him. She stumbled back a few steps and Markus didn't take his eyes off her. Not a person in the crowd said a word or moved an inch. My breath caught in my throat as she put the pieces together. Her mom stood and tried to push past me, but I held her back. She pushed harder, but my hold was firm. I knew she wanted to help her daughter right now, but Lilith had to figure this out for herself.

Lilith's gaze swept over the crowd. Tears dripped from her eyes as she took in everything and everyone around her.

When her eyes finally landed on me, they held longing. "You really didn't give up..."

I shook my head, moving to stand in front of her, laying my heart bare for her to see. "I would never give up on you, Lilith. I love you too damn much to do that."

"You wrote me letters?" she asked.

"Three hundred and twenty-seven of them, if I'm correct. Got a little carried away sometimes,." I chuckled, rubbing my forehead.

"You still love me?" she asked me.

I could almost see her brain racing to understand everything. "More than I did yesterday and less than I will tomorrow," I said, running my fingers down her face. A warmth spread across her cheeks at my admission, and a slow smile broke out across her lips.

"Alec?"

"Yes?"

"Can we both stop fighting this?" She bit her lip.

The grin that stretched across my face had light beaming from it. "With pleasure." I leaned down and placed my lips back where they have always belonged.

Chapter 27

Lilith

MY LIPS TANGLED with his in a searing kiss. Each movement sent chills down my spine and warmed my heart. It wasn't a mechanical kiss, one that you just went through the motions. It was an assurance, we fit perfectly together like the moment we stood in.

I clutched fistfuls of hair lightly in my hands as I pulled him closer to me. My heart, so broken and shattered, pieced back together like the last piece of a puzzle snapping into place. Flames shot up through the cracks, melding them all together so they'd never come apart again. I'd thought some things could never mend, but all I needed was Alec. He'd held the key all along. He'd known how to put me back together the whole time. He made me whole. I'd only had to accept it.

The world around us vanished, so lost in the moment nothing else mattered. I couldn't pay attention to the cries of outrage or disgust. I couldn't focus on the calls of the boys telling us we should get inside. It was only Alec and me in that moment, and nothing could take it away.

His lips disappeared from mine, and I forced my eyes open. His stared back at me and happiness danced through them, making them gleam. My hands let go of his hair and slid to his chest as I grinned up at him.

"Come with me?" he asked softly, a smile playing on his lips.

Any words I had in my head vanished. My brain and mouth wouldn't work together, so I nodded.

He took my hand and pulled me away from the chaos erupting around us. It was only then I fully opened my eyes to see what was happening. People stared at us, some happy and others angry. Arguments erupted all around us as I whipped my head around, looking at the place I'd just been led from. I tugged on Alec's hand, halting his movements, and he looked at me with pinched brows. I gave him a quick smile and kissed his cheek gently.

"Give me just a minute?" I asked, untangling my hand from his, turning to walk back to where we just stood. A sad smile rested on my lips as I approached a miserable looking Markus. He looked up at my approach and gazed at Alec before landing his eyes back upon me.

"Lilith?" he asked in a gentle voice.

Smiling softly and ignoring the question in his eyes, I stepped forward, wrapping my arms around him. He froze before leaning into my touch and enclosed me in a gentle embrace.

"Lilith?" he whispered into my ear.

"Thank you," I said softly into his.

He pulled back, looking at me with a dumbstruck look, eyes filled with confusion. Even though he had caused so much trouble and even caused me pain, I still saw his adoration. I'd always known it was there, but I'd thought he'd been as good of an actor as me. It had been his job, after all. Now, though, I realized I was wrong.

"Excuse me?" he asked, tilting his head to the side in question.

"Thank you. For letting me go...for not making me do this," I gestured to the scene around us.

He dropped his gaze to the ground. "As much as I wanted to, I—I couldn't make you go through with it," he whispered, picking at his black tux.

"I know, and as strange as this may sound, I'm not angry at you," I said.

"You're not?"

"No." Shaking my head with a chuckle, I leaned forward and placed a kiss on his cheek. "I think we both know if you hadn't let me go, I wouldn't be here in a few years' time. Maybe less..."

His soft brown eyes gazed into mine, understanding the depth of my confession. I may have been willing to get married and continue like nothing was wrong, but I never agreed to live, to continue my life. I knew deep in my heart I wouldn't have lasted a few more years. Every pain in my life would have doubled by then had I not been given the chance to be with Alec. He numbed the pain and made me feel alive again. He was the reason I could breathe again.

It had always been Alec I needed, and it would always be Alec I couldn't live without.

"Good luck—with you and Alec—I mean," he said, a genuine smile gracing his lips for the first time.

We hugged once more before I stepped away from him and turned around.

Alec stood there, waiting, a smile on his lips. He held his hand out to me, saying my name breathlessly. I wrapped my hand around Alec's, weaving my fingers with his as he led me away from my almost-wedding.

I didn't have a single regret. No remorse. Only happiness seeped through my veins so much it poured out of me. Every problem disappeared. The wall surrounding me dropped away, and in its place a shield formed, guarding me against negativity but letting the happiness through.

Alec was the happiness in my life. I had been incredibly blessed with a wonderful career, beautiful family, and lifelong friends, but none of it even held a flicker of emotion to what I felt for Alec. In this single moment, I didn't care what would happen to our careers next or what tomorrow might bring. Maybe that was selfish of me, but the warmth of Alec's body created a barrier and took all the thoughts away. I only thought of him. Nothing else.

***

"Alec, where the hell are we going? We've been driving for two hours." I groaned from the passenger's seat.

He only chuckled and shook his head, giving nothing away. We'd left the wedding two hours ago and had been on the road ever since.

He wouldn't tell me anything about where we were going or even why. He stayed silent the entire time, one hand driving and the other holding my hand in his lap.

He hadn't let go of me except when he climbed into the car. His thumb traced soothing patterns over my rough skin. Every few minutes, he lifted it to his lips and placed a burning kiss on my flesh. Goosebumps soared up my arms.

He smiled at me once more, and his eyes twinkled with mischief. He ignored my cries for answers. Sighing, I threw my head back against the headrest and gazed out the window.

"You think the whole world knows by now?" I asked, staring at the passing trees.

"Probably. I wouldn't be surprised if it were CG who let everyone know." he chuckled, looking over his shoulder to switch lanes on the highway.

"Why do you say that?" I shifted to be able to see him better.

"She had her phone out recording the whole damn thing. I'm surprised you didn't see it," he stated.

"What? No, she didn't!" I blanched at him, and he laughed at my embarrassed features. "What the hell is she going to do with it?"

"Blackmail? It's CG, do we ever actually know what she's thinking?" He laughed, his dimples poking out from his cheeks.

My eyes stayed locked on his gorgeous smile, dimples, and perfect lips. My free hand reached over to trace the edges around them, catching him off guard, but he smiled wider. My thumbs traced the outer lines of his bottom lip before dipping into his dimple.

"I missed these..." I breathed, not taking my gaze away. My thumb still tracing the contours of his lips and cheeks. Unwanted tears pooled in my eyes as memories came back to me. An ache shot through my heart thinking about all the moments we'd missed out on over the past few years. "Alec, I-" my breath caught in my throat, unable to push the words out as the tears slipped down my cheeks.

The car came to a sudden stop, and Alec to turn toward me. His hands cupped my face, bright eyes staring straight into my watery ones. His thumbs padded over my cheeks, catching the silent tears and he wiped them away.

"No apologies, Lilith," he said, stopping the words lodged in my throat.

I stared at him, more tears pouring out in place of the words I couldn't find. Every tear that slipped down my cheek was a silent apology. I hated myself for letting everything fall apart the way it had. My tears told him that. I'd let him slip through my fingers when I could have stopped it all. I could have demanded we stay together, I could have saved our friendship at the very least, but instead, I did nothing. I killed his soul, stepped on it like it was dirt, like it meant nothing to me.

The tears poured out faster than he could catch as sobs wracked my body. I would never be able to get the past few years back. Even if we stayed together for the rest of our lives, I could never take back the pain I had caused him. Day by day, I had only made it worse, and I wanted nothing more than to make it all disappear like it had never happened, but that would never be a possibility.

"Lil, please, don't cry." He pulled my sobbing body against his.

His hand brushed through my hair while his other one rubbed my back.

I thought back to everything that had happened since we were torn apart, and to everything that happened in the past year. Since that terrible night I'd decided to take my own life. I'd made an urgent decision to end the pain and sorrow that I felt daily in hopes it would not only make everything in my life better, but also Alec's. Some sick part of me felt that he would find happiness in my death, a release. I knew now he wouldn't have, but my sickened mind had truly believed it.

For so long, I took everything out on myself. Scars marred my body not only in the form of tattoos but also the ones I created myself. Burns, scrapes, cuts, anything I could find to inflict pain on me in hopes it would relieve Alec's.

It was so easy to take the pills that night, to step into the water and let them lull me to sleep. It was so easy to drag the blade across my skin and watch as the blood slipped effortlessly from the cut. It was so easy to say goodbye to everyone I cared about when they weren't in front of me, but it was hard once I started to dream of Alec. I saw him as the pills pulled me into the darkness; he was there, my light, begging me to hold on for a few more moments.

"I can't," my drug-induced mind had screamed at him. For some reason, I kept fighting. My brain knew there was no use in struggling against the vast number of pills I had swallowed, but my heart told me otherwise.

Strangely, I had hoped Alec had been watching that night. I knew he would, but there was always the chance he would have been fed up by then. Somewhere deep inside, I had silently prayed for him to save me. I had planned out everything, but maybe, just maybe, if he'd wanted me, he'd somehow be my knight in shining armor. My hero. He'd figure out a way. How stupid was that?

"It wasn't a coincidence," my voice was raspy against the silence inside the car. I couldn't see anything around us but trees. My head was still cradled against Alec's chest, listening to the beating of his heart.

"What wasn't, babe?" he asked, placing a kiss on the top of my head.

"The room number," the words came out as an exhale. "When I got to the room, I warred within my head. I wanted to leave and run to you, yet I really wanted to die," I said sadly.

"Lilith, I don't—"

"No, Alec, I need to say this" I cut him off, looking up from my spot on his chest. "When I sat down to start the live feed on my camera, I wanted to give you some way to help me, but you'd have to figure it out."

"I'm not sure I understand." He pulled me to sit up and look at him. "What are you talking about?"

"The room number...that's why I said I only had that much time left. I was trying to give you some sort of insight or something, to help you find me, leaving it up to fate I guess..." I shrugged, looking down at my hands.

"Oh, Lil." He placed a finger beneath my chin and lifted my gaze. "You have no idea how happy I am you did that. I was going crazy. I couldn't figure out how to help you, to stop you from leaving me."

"I'm sorry," I whispered.

He shook his head. "No apologies, babe." He smiled. "It's a new start from here, okay? Everything else is in the past. It's time to live for now and to live for us."

"I just thought you would want to know everything," I said to him, lost for words.

"I do, babe, and I have the rest of my life to learn and listen to everything, but for now, I want to spend time with you and forget about everything else." He smiled, leaning forward to peck my lips lightly before he pulled back, opening his door and stepping out. When he pulled away, I looked out at the scenery before us and saw a secluded cabin settled deep in the trees. My door opened, Alec's hand tugging on my own as he pulled me out of the car.

"Alec?" I asked, looking around us.

He smiled brightly at me, placing his hands on my hips as he stood behind me. "This," he nodded his head toward the cabin. "This is for us for the next two days. No media, no meetings, no interruptions." His lips grazed the nick of my neck.

"Just us?" I asked, my breathing picking up slightly.

"I want to...reconnect. I've lost too much time." His lips trailed a hot spiral down the course of my neck, his hands gripping my hips and pulling them back against him.

"Then let's make up for it," I groaned in my lust-filled haze.

A weekend away with only Alec and me, to relearn everything

we may have forgotten. My body and mind called out to learn the curves of his body once again, to make him writhe in pleasure underneath me. It wasn't so much to make up for lost time but to be together in the moment, a moment we'd both waited so long to have again.

"Just one thing," he smirked at me.

My eyes widened as I swallowed the lump in my throat. "What's that?" I asked breathlessly.

"Since when did I ever let you lead?"

Chapter 28

Lilith

"ALEC, FORTHE last time, you wait until it starts to bubble before flipping it over," I huffed dramatically as I watched Alec attempt to flip yet another pancake.

He ignored my directions again and flipped it to early, tearing the entire pancake apart.

"Dammit!" he muttered, jutting his lip out into a cute pout I would have taken in between my teeth if I weren't starved.

"At this rate, we'll never eat," I groaned, letting my head fall onto the sleek countertop.

After arriving yesterday, we had barely slept, and had managed to keep ourselves completely naked the entire time. It was only now, at four in the afternoon, I had put a stop to the constant touching and kissing because I needed sustenance if this continued. I had no clue how he kept his energy up, but mine had been gone for quite some time. And I wouldn't get it back unless he learned how to make a freaking pancake.

"How the hell have you managed to keep yourself fed over the past three years?" I chuckled, lifted myself off the barstool, and strutted over to where he stood glaring at the pan. I took the spatula from his hand and gently nudged him aside.

"Take out?" He scratched the back of his neck. "I just wanted to make you something to eat," he frowned.

A smile graced my lips as I turned my head to place a light kiss on the corner of his mouth. His eyes met mine with a fraction of embarrassment and lust. "I know, but maybe we should eat now and teach you how to cook later?" I chuckled at the blush spreading over his cheeks.

He nodded sheepishly and leaned forward to place his hands on top of my bony hips and watched me make us each a stack of pancakes. "How'd you learn to cook anyways?" His chin rested atop my shoulder.

"When you live in a house with a chef, you learn quickly. Not many girly things to do when both your parents are chefs at a top-end restaurant." I said, shrugging. I still smiled at the fond memories of the late-night talks with mom. Her laughter flooded my mind, and I realized just how much time I'd lost with my parents as well. Having ignored my family mostly because I couldn't bear for them to find out what was truly happening with me.

"Well, apparently, I missed the cooking class with my mom," he huffed.

"Yeah, she left me with a lot of work to do," I grinned up at him, holding back a chuckle.

He glared but with a gleam of amusement lighting the corners of his eyes. "Are you upset by that, Lil?"

"Nope, I like a challenge, just never thought I would have to teach my boy—" my voice faltered and cut off, my eyes widened at the words I almost let slip past my lips. My gaze dropped down to the sizzling pan in front of me, but I still felt his eyes on me.

I quickly brushed past him to grab the plates and placed our simple pancakes on them. I tried to distract myself as Alec made his way to stand behind me. His body radiated heat I could feel even though he wasn't touching me.

"Lilith?" he asked.

I ignored him. "Four pancakes enough?" I gritted my teeth, handing him his plate.

He took it, setting it on the countertop before turning back to me. His hands gripped my waist, spinning me around to face him, but my gaze stayed locked on my feet. "Babe?" he asked me again, trying to lift my chin to meet his piercing eyes, but I looked everywhere except for at him. "What were you going to say?"

I shook my head, shrugging my shoulders in indifference. I knew this situation would float to the surface at some point, but I didn't think it would be so soon. I had ruined the perfect bubble around us, already trying to place a label on our relationship. Alec may have only wanted this weekend together, not a lifetime. I knew I wanted more than just a few shags over the span of two days, but that was only me. He had always been so hard to read, and even to this day that still hadn't changed.

"Lilith..." he breathed out in warning, agitation making its way into his tone. "Talk to me."

My eyes danced up to his, and I considered his words. "It was nothing, Alec...please just eat, okay?" I mumbled.

I took a step away from him, grabbing my plate and setting it on top of the counter. Sitting on a barstool, I ignored Alec's heated gaze boring into my back. I played with my food, stabbing it with my fork, unable to place any in my mouth under so much scrutiny. Sighing, I stood and moved out of the room and away from his strong gaze.

"Where are you going?" Alec asked, calculating my every move.

"I'm not hungry anymore. I think I'll just take a shower." Without waiting for his response, I made my way down the hall into the master bedroom.

I wasn't sure how Alec had found this place, but he had outdone himself. The cabin had the feel of being secluded with no one to bother us, yet it didn't make me feel isolated. The moment we stepped inside, a calming sense of peace washed over me, like I'd come home. Of course, anywhere Alec was would always feel like home, but I was comfortable here.

The logs around the outside of the cabin matched seamlessly with the insides. Large windows framed the walls, but with so much privacy it only let the sunlight inside, spreading warmth and light. One large bed dotted the house in the master suite along with a bathtub big enough to fit a massive football team. I walked into the huge expanse of the bathroom and my eyes fell onto the bathtub sitting in the corner where just mere hours ago I had laid with Alec. The boy was determined to mark every space in the entire cabin, hence the need to eat. My stomach was growling in protest, but I couldn't go back down to face him yet.

I was so embarrassed. I'd almost slipped and said boyfriend. I knew he'd caught it, but I couldn't bring myself to ask him how he felt about the word. I didn't need a label, but I'd dreamed of Alec that way for so long it just slipped. It had always been so natural for us to fall into place with each other. We never bothered with labels before, but for some reason, it bothered me now. I wanted the label; I wanted to know I was his and he was mine. I needed it, and I craved it.

Steam filled the bathroom, hot water pelting my bare skin as thoughts consumed me. Eyes closed and head against the shower wall, I thought of everything we had done in the last twenty-four hours. Every touch, kiss, and sound still lingered on my skin, branding me.

I was sure I had never seen Alec like this. So needy and primal, but I wasn't one to complain. He had shown me how much he craved me, but even more, he showed me how much he loved me. The words had slipped past his sweet lips more times than I could count, but each time, they hammered further into my heart. I would never grow tired of hearing those words from him because each time he said them, they sounded sweeter, and I found my body waiting to hear what they would sound like the next time.

Muddled thoughts clouded my mind so much I hadn't heard the door to the shower open. Cool hands snaked over my hips, and I jumped. My eyes opened as a gasp escaped my throat. I tilted to see my intruder.

"Okay if I join?" He grinned at me, already knowing I would never deny him.

I wanted to smile and play along, but my confidence faltered, and my gaze dropped to the floor. I studied our feet, water swirling around them as he pulled my body flush against his, back to chest.

"Lilith," he whispered hotly into my ear. "Please tell me you're not upset about what you said."

My teeth sunk into my bottom lip.

"I'm not mad, babe," he said, lips moving over the shell of my ear, tongue darting out as he nipped the tender skin.

I shivered. "I—I didn't mean to say anything. I'm sorry." Hot, short pants of air fell from my lips while his trailed down my neck slowly, teasingly.

"I'm not sorry," he smirked against my skin when he placed his lips on just the right spot to cause a moan to push past my closed lips. "That's what I want to be, Lil, your boyfriend, anything, just as long as it's with you."

Large hands moved over my abdomen as kisses continued their sweet torture down the length of my neck. I could already feel myself twitching with desire, every bone in my body aching to meld with him. I couldn't help what his words did to me, the effect they had on me. The physical relationship between Alec and me had always been shared equally. Sometimes he was in control, and other times I sought dominance. He thought because of our height difference he could tower over me and make me beg for things to be his way. While in some situations it would be all I ever wanted, to be led in submission on my knees for him. Tonight was different. His words lit something deep inside of me, turning on a switch I hadn't experienced yet. I could picture everything I wanted to do with this boy, forever. I wanted to see his eyes closed together tightly, fighting off the screams of pleasure. I wanted to hear him chant my name over and over again. I had waited so long for these moments. Even though we had been together for over twenty-four hours, it still felt like the first time.

***

My eyes focused on Alec laying on the bed, eyes wide and boring straight into mine. A lustful haze crossed them as I slowly sauntered over to him, drinking in the sight of him waiting for me. His long, lean, and beautifully smooth skin waited to have my lips pouring over them. Each tattoo waited to be traced by my tongue and blown over with warm breath. Every part of him screamed out to be touched, and yet I just wanted to stare at him all day.

"Lil..." he cried softly, impatience dripping into his tone.

My body moved at the sound of him calling my name. In seconds, I hovered over him, staring down. My eyes gazed at every contour of his delicate face, and I was hit with the force of just how much I loved him. It was a defining moment for me. I'd always known I loved him, but it slammed into me so hard I didn't have a clue how much until right now.

Emotion overtook my body, and tears gathered in my eyes. I felt ridiculous at the fact we were both lying in bed with our naked bodies pressed together, need and lust burning between us, and yet I was crying.

His brows creased together. "Babe? What's wrong?" He rubbed the pads of his thumbs under my eyes, catching every tear that dared to escape. "We don't have to do this if you don't want to, love."

I smiled at his sincerity, knowing full well he would never expect anything out of me other than what I desired. Never would he force me into doing something I didn't want or wasn't capable of doing.

"No, that's not it." Shaking my head, I lowered it, pressing our foreheads against each other and closing my eyes. "I just love you, Alec, so much, and I—"

"I love you too, Lilith," he said. Simple and to the point.

"I still can't believe I have you back. I've dreamed about this for so long it almost doesn't feel real. I don't want to wake up to you gone, Alec. So many nights I cried and begged for you, but I knew I couldn't have you. So many times, I took it out on myself because it was the only way I could get a grip on reality." My eyes fluttered open to gaze into his saddened ones. "I'm sorry for everything. I know you said no apologies, but you need to know how sorry I am, how much I regret listening to my doubts, how much I wish I could go back and change everything, but I can't, and I can only make the best of today and our future."

Slowly, a smile spread across his lips as he leaned up to place a soft kiss on mine. He shifted us both into a sitting position, and I straddled his waist, but the moment was too strong to be driven by sexual desires. Love and understanding settled between us, and although I wasn't sure what he was doing, I still felt at peace. He dropped his gaze to look down to where my hands rested on his chest. With slow and languid movements, he picked up my left hand and placed his own on it, intertwining our fingers. With a gentle squeeze, he turned my arm over, revealing a mixture of body art in all different forms. Raised flesh, marred skin, and ink all rested upon my arm. His fingers gently traced them, causing me to gasp at the intensity of the moment.

"Alec," I said firmly, trying to pull my arm from his reach. I didn't want him to see the ugly skin on my body, the moments I broke down and resorted to something I would never be proud of.

"I love you, Lilith. I always have, and I plan to love you forever." His head lowered to our locked hands, and he placed a kiss on the side of my palm. "Everything that has happened to us may not have been what we'd planned, but it brought us where we are today. We're together." A single kiss placed upon theraised skin where a blade had first cut it open. "Every scar you see as an imperfection," he kissed over a burn mark from a cigarette lighter, "I see as an accomplishment." He raised his eyes.

"Accomplishment?" I asked, not sure what he could mean by that.

He nodded, lowering his head to a tattoo. "Yes. An accomplishment showing how far you've come. These are scars, Lil. Things of the past, not the present. If there are no new ones, then yes, they are accomplishments." His eyes burned into mine with a heated and heavy understanding. "I wish I could change all the ways you hurt yourself before, but I can't. All I can do is be proud of you for how far you've come. And I am, baby. I'm so proud."

My cheeks heated up, but the rush of tears cooled them instantly. His hands left my arms to grasp my face and look at me as his own tears shimmered in his eyes.

"I love you, Alec," I said, receiving a nod from him.

"Show me."

That was all he had to whisper before I planted my lips on his.

No more words of declaration were needed as I pushed him down onto the mattress. Nothing but love and understanding floated between us with every simmering kiss, every rough and gentle touch. Our hands roamed and explored each other's bodies like newfound territory. My palms glided up and down the muscles of his torso and down the sides of his hips and legs. Bodies tangled and intertwined together, loving each other the right way.

Words could say a lot between two people, but actions showed it all. Some people said sex could never show someone how much you loved them, but when it happened between two people who loved each other as we did, power rested within it. It became passion. Adoration. It became more than love. Something I could never find the words to describe. But, I knew one thing. It was something I'd never, ever give up. Not for anything in this world.

Epilogue

Alec

PEOPLE SAID THAT gravity kept us all on the ground. A force that held us down, so we didn't float away. The only problem was that I didn't believe in that crap anymore. My sense of gravity didn't come from some man centuries ago telling me how and why my ass stayed here on earth. I was bound by something far greater than a form of science. The cables that knit me to the earth weren't the work of some greater force. It was simply love. Love from the most important person in my world kept me here, and kept me centered and gravitating toward the earth. Lilith was my gravity.

Word of Lilith's and my relationship spread quickly. The media ate it up, and the fans took to it wholeheartedly. I'd be lying if I said everyone accepted us because that was simply not the case. The majority stayed by our sides and supported us, more than we had ever expected. But there were still those who ridiculed us. Some of it

251

had been rather harsh, and it had taken Lilith by surprise more than it had me.

She hadn't handled it as well as she could have, but I was always there by her side to guide her and try to protect her. The other band members were as well, always there to shield her from pain as much as we could. Two of our biggest supporters were CG and Jase, simply because they were experiencing the same thing. But like all things, it eventually passed. People started to see how much we loved each other, and others started to appreciate that we were proud of who we were, and there wasn't a damn thing they could do about it.

Over time, we moved on and just continued our careers the same way we would have if Lilith and I not been together. With a new team behind us and stronger fans than we had thought possible, our careers were at the top of the world again, and we couldn't be happier.

Two years had passed since the day I had finally gotten my Lilith back. Two years of learning each other all over again and rebuilding a friendship. It had been the best two years of both of our lives. A day didn't pass that we weren't smiling or we weren't saying we loved each other. We seemed to have grown to impossible heights, and I would never tire of that.

Lately, I thought it might be time to take the next step. Taking our relationship even further excited me, but it also scared the crap out of me. I'd spent weeks sitting in our newly purchased home thinking of how the hell I could ask her to marry me but came up with nothing. Every time I thought I'd come up with an idea, panic made the breath rush from my body. Needless to say, I backed out.

Every time.

"Stop overanalyzing it, Alec," I heard a groan from beside me and turned to look at the person next to me. Jase sat there with his head laid back against the couch and his face in a scowl. "It's not that hard."

"That's easy for you to say, you're already married," I huffed at him, crossing my arms over my chest. All I got in return was a massive grin from the newlywed beside me. I rolled my eyes and pushed myself off the couch. "Don't rub it in, asshole."

"Sorry... I can't help it," he smiled sheepishly.

Jase and CG had gotten married two months ago and were the epitome of happiness. They had been together much longer than any of us knew, but all of us were still surprised when Jase asked CG to marry him. It was a massive celebration. Family, friends, and our team all came together to show their love and support for the couple. As happy as I was for them, I also wanted to shove both of them six feet under.

"Not helping, Jase. How did you do it again?" I asked him, taking small steps to look out of the large window in our living room.

"Alec, I've told you a million times," he groaned. "We were on our yearly vacation, and I just did it. No big production." He shrugged it off. "But yours doesn't have to be the same."

Groaning, I turned to face him and nodded. I sighed and sat back down, placing my face into my hands and basking in the silence around us. My mind swirled with ideas, but none of them seemed to be good enough for Lilith. She deserved better than the best, and it felt like everything I came up with would only ever be mediocre. A single chime from my phone broke the silence in the room. Digging it out of my pocket, I looked up to see Jase smirking down at his phone, and I rolled my eyes at him. Dirty bastard couldn't even help me for thirty minutes without blushing or smirking at something from his conversations with CG. A smile broke out onto my lips at the simple "I love you" text I received from Lilith. Things like that could always make anything bad or stressful fade away. My stress relief was interrupted when my front door rammed open, and an out of breath CG and Jaxson came rushing inside.

"Alec," Jaxson shouted at me, and I stood up, looking at him confused. "Get your laptop."

My eyes widened at his words. Those words alone sent me back three years ago to a night I wanted to forget more than anything.

"Jax, are you fucking sick?" I whispered to him, placing a hand over my heart

He shook his head, his eyes pleading and begging me to listen. "I am serious Alec. I-Its Lilith..."

I stood there gaping at him, not sure what to do next until CG stood up and handed me an already turned on MacBook with Lilith's face brightly lit up on the screen. I stared at it in wonder and confusion, my body slumping back onto the couch feeling lifeless once again.

"Lilith?" I whispered, as a nervous jolt crept under my skin.

"It's okay, Alec," she smiled at me, and it was only then that I realized we were both connected through Skype. "You look scared.

What happened to being—what did you call yourself again? Oh right, 'bad to the bone'?" she chuckled as she raised an eyebrow.

"Well, this is a bit too familiar for my liking." I frowned, not a trace of happiness coming from me.

"I know, but I'm hoping to change that," she winked.

I tilted my head to the side. My eyes roamed the screen, but I couldn't get a good look at her surroundings. Only a small stream behind her was visible. Her face shined bright, happiness gleaming from every feature.

"What do you mean?" I asked her, noticing the sundress she was wearing with flowers in her hair. "Where are you?"

"You said this was a bit too familiar, right?" she ignored my last question, but I nodded my head. "I don't want to bring up the past, to ever hurt you, Alec. I love you more than I could ever begin to express. But, I don't want you to always live in fear for us. I know you still think that one day we're going to end. That I'm going to leave you."

My eyes fell to my lap. Her words rang true. Too true. But I didn't want to admit it.

"You never have to fear that, Alec. Yes, I was once in a very dark place, but you brought me out of that. It was always you, Alec; no one else deserves the credit for my recovery except *you*."

"Why tell me like this?" I asked, my eyebrows pinching together.

She just grinned. "Do you remember the first few weeks after we got signed? When we all got to go home for a short while, and I went on vacation to Paris with my family, so we Skyped every night?" she asked me, and I couldn't help but grin as I nodded, remembering all the nightly Skype sessions. "We learned a lot about each other during those few weeks of video chatting. Then three years ago we had a different form of it. It was the night I told the world how I felt about you. How much I loved and adored you but couldn't have you. Although you couldn't talk back to me, I knew you were watching."

"Okay, but I still don't understand what that has to do with now?"

"I'm getting there, love," she chuckled softly. "A few monumental moments in our lives have come from this stupid video thing. A lot of it good, but some bad, yet still important parts of our lives. I want to add another good memory to that, one that I hope will outweigh any bad memories you have of us and replace them with something you can remember until the day we die, old and gray, together."

I bit my lip as she looked down, moving her arms over the camera to reach for something. When her gaze met mine and her hands returned in front of her, a gasp escaped my lips. A lazy smile rested on her lips as she lifted a small black box in her hand.

"Lilith..." I whispered, completely mesmerized by the moment.

"Alec, from the second I met you, I knew you and I would have a special relationship. I didn't know exactly what type, but I knew you would be a part of my life forever. It wasn't just about the band or the careers we would have together. It was about how you made me feel. Every smile and laugh you gave me made my heart ten times bigger than before I met you. You've always meant so much to me, and even when we went through our worst times together, I loved you more than I did the first time I ever spoke those words to you." She took a deep breath while I continued to hold mine, tears blurring my vision at her words.

"Alec, you're my forever, but I can't have you for forever unless you say you want us to be together as well. I want to marry you. I want to have a life together, kids together, everything you can imagine. I want it with you. So, Alec..." She smiled sweetly through the camera as she opened the box. "Will you marry me?"

Her question took my breath away. Everything around me turned to darkness, and all I saw in front of me was Lilith. Everything I had ever wanted in life led me to this moment, this beautiful moment. A moment so precious, only Lilith would ever be able to create. Tears streamed down my cheeks, but with her, I didn't care how girly I came off. And I knew she didn't care either.

"Yes," I spoke through an exhale, smiling widely through my tears and receiving the brightest smile in return. I couldn't believe what she had just done. *She asked me to marry her.*

It was at that moment something in the box caught my eyes and caused me to frown in confusion.

"Hold on, I don't understand. Why are there two rings?" I asked her, confused.

"One is an engagement ring; your mother insisted I use your grandmother's ring for myself, but the other two are wedding rings," she stated. "I don't want to wait to marry you. I don't want to take the time planning something elaborate when all I care about is you saying *I do,* and me saying it back." She stood up, lifting the camera and turning it around to show me what was in front of her and out of my line of vision.

Now facing the camera, I saw both of our families standing behind her, dressed up with big smiles adorning each of their faces. A few chairs lined the lawn, and in the background, I saw a table and tent set up. But most importantly, standing there waving like idiots were CG, in a violet dress to match her now violet hair, and Jase and Jaxson dressed up in suits. I had never even heard them sneak out.

"Wait, Lilith, where are you?" I suddenly asked, confused as the screen shifted back to her.

"At our wedding," she said with a small smile on her face. "In the garden beside our house."

She didn't have to say another word. I jumped out of my seat, turned, and ran out the door. Something hanging over the chair to my right glimmered in the sunlight. A black suit laid across it and I slowed down to grab it. A note fell from it to the ground, and I bent down and picked it up, eyeing it carefully.

Hurry up and get changed, you big goober!

I love you.

x Lil x

"I'm waiting, babe," I heard Lilith chuckle behind me through the still opened laptop.

That was all it took. I rushed up the stairs and into our bedroom. That was how it had always been with Lilith and me. We weren't ones to need a huge wedding to show the world we loved each other. All we needed was us. Lilith knew me inside and out; she knew all I ever needed was a simple wedding. Not the stress of planning something elaborate, but only her, our families, and our closest friends.

I always dreamed of the moment I waited at the end of the aisle for Lilith to meet me. At one point, I thought that dream was taken away from me. But, it was returned in the sweetest way. Lilith was my past, present, and now my future. Nothing could or ever would take her away. My heart hammered in my chest, the movement so loud it made my ears pound. I stood, staring into the floor length mirror. My black tux fit perfectly around my body. The deep purple tie tied everything together. A soft white rose that matched the ones I saw in her hair earlier was pinned neatly against the lapel of my tuxedo jacket. Lilith had done a perfect job picking it out for me, not like I expected any less from her.

I couldn't wrap my mind around what was about to take place. In just a few simple minutes, my life would change. Lilith had already become the center of my entire universe, but I knew that all along this was what I truly wanted: to be married to the love of my life, to have that everlasting tie with her. The strings of my heart reached out to her and looped together with hers for the rest of eternity.

No, I didn't need a simple piece of paper that could be washed away at any moment to declare my love for Lilith. It was more than a documentation or declaration to the world. It was more than just a few words said in a ceremony. To me, it was everything I had ever wanted. To be completely devoted to Lilith in every way possible. To be able to look at her hand and see a symbol of our love there. To sneak glances of love and adoration, at her side forever. It would be the very core of my being and would be the glue that held us together. Forever.

With our marriage, we'd have to face a lot more trials. I knew that. People would ridicule us. Shame us. Or try to...but none of that mattered. It never had and it never would. I couldn't care less what the rest of the world thought. In my world, only Lilith and those who loved and accepted us existed. The ones who couldn't wrap their heads around us, who couldn't accept us—they didn't need to be a part of our lives.

With all the emotions and the excitement building inside of me, I had stood there in front of the mirror gawking at myself. I needed to move away from it and go to the gardens. She was there, waiting for me. A beautiful smile probably lined her face, but I couldn't get my feet to move. They were tied to the ground with steel cables that wouldn't let me move an inch. My heart beat so fast in my chest I was almost sure the only way I would be moving anytime soon was via a paramedic.

"Alec?" my mother's soft voice rang out from the doorway.

My eyes found hers, and the only thing I could see in them was sheer happiness. My mom's love for Lilith and her acceptance of us as a couple had never been a secret, nor had she ever shied away from the fact that she wanted us together. She knew the happiness it brought me, and in turn, brought her even more.

"Why are you still standing in here?" she asked as she stepped closer to me.

"I—I can't move?" I said in a questioning tone, shaking my head at how ridiculous I must sound. All the nerves fluttered to the surface at once, and I could barely speak.

"You know, I remember the day you brought Lilith home to

meet the family." She moved to stand in front of me, fixing my tie, so it was perfectly straight. "Of course, we had all met her before, but this was different. This was you bringing home your girlfriend, and I remember how nervous you were. Your eyes were constantly looking around to make sure everyone was happy and accepted her, but most importantly you stayed right by her side, never once letting her feel uncomfortable or alone." She smiled, looking directly into my eyes. "I could tell right then that this was your forever; she would be your forever, and I can't begin to explain the happiness I felt in my heart."

"Where are you going with this, Mom?" I asked her teasingly, and she only smiled bigger.

"My point is that you love her Alec, you always have. You've been through so much that I wish I could take away the pain both of you have had to live through, but I can't. The only thing I can do is tell you to hold on to her tight, Alec. Cherish the love you have with her every day of your lives and never let go. This is Lilith, the love of your life, the only reason you choose to exist today still, and as long as you remember that, you'll never live a day of unhappiness."

A full grin broke onto my face at her words as they settled deep in my heart. My arms reached out, pulling her into a hug as I held the one person who had always been the foundation of my life. Tears sprung into my eyes, but I forced them to remain at bay as I pulled away, giving her a soft kiss on the cheek. "Thank you, for everything." I took her hand and squeezed.

She nodded. "My babies are my greatest joy, and I'm thrilled Lilith will forever be a part of that. Now, let's go get you married

261

before she thinks she ran you off!" She smiled, pulling me out of the room with her small, yet strong, frame.

We walked silently out of the house and down to the gardens. The sight before me almost took my breath away. Every flower and plant had been elegantly groomed with even more added to the venue. Lights hung everywhere, and tables had been covered with white linen cloths. People grinned at me as I walked past, nodding their heads in congratulations. But what stood at the end of the garden knocked the wind from me.

White chairs were lined perfectly with all of our friends and family, who turned to stare at me. Everyone had dressed up in his or her best clothes and smiles of adoration adorned every face. But none of that caught my eye. I looked past my family, friends, and colleagues, and saw the one person that meant the most out of anyone in the world.

Lilith.

She stood there, smiling brightly, tears shining in her eyes as she watched me move toward her. It was all I could do not to run straight for her, pick her up, and kiss her breathless. Her beautiful white flowy sundress wrapped around her limb, outlining each contour of her body. The smirk on her face showed she knew the thoughts that ran through my mind.

My feet finally made their way to stand in front of her, only then noticing that my mom had left my side and I now stood alone. I didn't waste another moment, joining hands with Lilith. My head turned and took in the scene behind us, and I couldn't help the tear that slipped down my cheek. This was the moment I had dreamed about for so long. I never wanted some big and elaborate wedding but just a simple ceremony with those closest to us.

"Alec?"

I glanced over to see Lilith staring at me with a scrunched forehead.

"Are you alright, babe?"

"I'm perfect," I whispered. "Just happy and surprised. I think we have just broken every barrier known to man."

She smiled even bigger at knowing she managed to surprise me. My eyes fixed on hers; I only saw love and a happiness we now both shared in so many ways.

"Today we come together to unite two people as one. It's not a matter of a statement or declaration to the world as it is of bringing two hearts joined in love. Today Lilith and Alec stand before their closest family and friends to unite themselves together, finally, as a married couple."

My eyes looked over at the man speaking the words, seeing him smile toward both of us.

"Something as great as a love like yours isn't something to be kept quiet or to be ashamed of. It's something that should make you proud. Proud of everything you've accomplished and been through together. No great love comes without trial or pain, but it's those who love each other through it all that come out stronger, like you." His eyes looked over to Lilith, and I followed suit.

"Lilith, let's start with your vows."

Lilith smiled with a nod and looked over, her eyes searching mine. She quieted down for a moment in her search for words until she found she was looking to say and smiled before she took a deep breath and began.

"I've known I loved you from the moment first I laid eyes on you. As cheesy as that may sound, it's the truth. Every day since I was sixteen, you were the first thing I would think of when I woke up and the last thing on my mind as I drifted to sleep." She paused, looking down at our hands. "Alec, you're everything to me. Somehow you managed to sneak your way into my heart, and no matter what life brought us, you never left. I've never been more grateful for a single person in my life, and I've never loved someone as much as I love you. The years we've been together in happiness are nothing compared to what's to come. I'll love you until the day I die, and I promise—" she stopped, looking sternly into my tear-filled eyes, "that won't be until we're both old and ready to die together."

Tears made their way down my cheeks, and Lilith lifted one hand to brush them away with her thumb. The moment she started speaking, my whole body shook. I hadn't prepared anything. Had no idea what I'd say. Anxiety constricted my chest, making it almost impossible to breathe. But, looking down, I realized she didn't have a paper. She'd spoken from the heart, not from a memorized script. Every word she spoke was with sincerity and love. My own heart swelled with love, joy, and happiness when she said her words. Her stern promise to never leave me had made the tears flow. Mostly because I knew she'd meant it. We'd never again, put each other through any sort of pain. And I'd never let her go, never lose her. I knew that now. And that was the only reassurance I needed.

"Alec, would you like to say your vows?" The officiator asked, and I nodded.

I took a deep breath, ready to tell her exactly how I felt. "Lilith, I can honestly say I didn't expect this…I didn't expect our *unique* wedding day, but I can honestly say that out of everything that's happened in my life, none of it compares to the moment I met you. I'll never forget the feeling I had when I saw you, or the feeling I continued to have, the one that has grown every day, even now. I feel so safe, secure, and in love with you, and it is so different from anything else I have ever encountered. You became my world, the center of my universe, and that both terrified and thrilled me at the same time. I was terrified because I wasn't sure at that time what it meant or how to handle it, but I was also thrilled because it felt like I had found the one person that would change my life forever. Lil, I hope you know how so incredibly proud of you I am." I shook my head, letting out a small chuckle of astonishment.

"You are quite literally the strongest person I know, to have been through everything you've gone through. Never for a moment in my life have I ever regretted anything with you, and if being here with you today, so in love and happy, meant I would have to endure it all again, then I would. You have shown me so much devotion and love that I still wake up every day, shocked anyone could love me that much, yet you do. I want to cherish and love you for the rest of our lives and spend every day showing you how much you mean to me and how happy I am that you're still here with me." My eyes searched hers as my mouth opened to pour out every emotion I felt.

The tears and sounds coming from both of us and friends and family would be almost comical if not for this precious moment wrapped around us. My arms were aching to wrap around her and hold her, but I forced them to stay at my sides and stared at her face. The face I'd get to wake up to every morning and fall asleep beside every night. The beautiful face that I'd get to keep as my most prized possession.

"Lilith, do you take Alec to be the only one you devote yourself to, love, cherish and be honest with for the rest of your life?" The man asked Lilith, a smile evident in his voice.

"I do." Lilith grinned at me.

"And do you, Alec, take Lilith to be the only one you devote yourself to, love, cherish and be honest with for the rest of your life?"

"I do." I smiled back instantly.

"Hell yeah, you do!" was shouted from the crowd.

We turned around to see CG fist pumping, a smile on her face as everyone laughed and agreed with her.

"Well, it's my pleasure and honor to now declare you both as husband and wife, united in love. You may seal it with a kiss."

My body instantly reacted, and my arms couldn't stand the thought of not having her wrapped around me any longer. I grabbed her by the waist, pulling her to me and swiftly placed my lips on hers and pulled her as close to me as humanly possible. She eagerly returned the gesture, grabbing onto the lapels of my jacket and holding me to her as our lips moved in sync.

Every day of my life, even before I met Lilith, was just in

anticipation of this very moment. The moment we became the Youngs, our love united. Never would another moment be as special or endearing as this one, when I had the only person I'd ever managed to love wrapped in my arms and securely there to stay forever.

We may have once been apart or thought we'd lose each other, but an undeniable pull always brought us back together. Our hearts were forever tied to each other with a love that could never be broken.

Like all things, *happiness* came with time.

Note From the Author

Dear Reader,

Today the world is losing its human interaction factor. We see the world through a screen and believe everything we read or see on the internet because it couldn't possibly be false. Remember that just because everything seems normal doesn't mean it really is.

Depression is a serious condition that can only be treated if we allow it to be.

Suicide attempts in teens and young adults are at an all-time high; you can easily miss cries for help if you aren't looking closely enough. Be aware and watch for the signs, because what happened in this book could have easily gone the other way.

So, the next time you get on social media, remember this book and how that words can easily change lives if we are not careful with how we use them.

For all the Lilith's and Alec's in the world, I see you and you are not alone.

Much Love,

H. L. Roberts

A c k n o w l e d g e m e n t s

The journey for this book started a long time before the actual writing took place and long before publishing it was even an option. Some might say that it took an entire army to get this book published.

To my family who taught me to love like a blind person, with my eyes closed my heart open, I will be eternally grateful. All of your support during this process is the only reason I was able to make it through the endless amount of editing and rewrites. Mom, you were right, it was worth the wait.

To the incredible people who taught me three valuable lessons that I will never forget. *Mr. Cross*, you took the time and gave me the second chance that no one else did. You taught me what true friendship meant and that the second grade really can be fun. *Mrs. Walker*, you taught me that the best adventures could come by simply going to the library to have afternoon tea with the Mad Hatter, going to far off adventures in a treehouse, and all of the cool kids lived with their siblings in an abandoned train car. You gave me the love for the fictional world and have forever changed my life. *Mrs. Rushing*, you taught me my biggest life lesson; that anything is possible with a little hard work, dedication, and the stubbornness to never give up.

Cassandra Fear, you have become my rock in this industry. Thank you for becoming my best friend and pushing me when I started to crumble.

271

About the Author

H. L. Roberts is a writer from a small Kentucky town. She comes from a big family, and often finds herself sitting with them around the television watching movies, and just staying close. This is how she believes a family should be.

Reading is one of her passions, and so is advocating for metnal illnesses, as well as epilepsy. She wants to bring awareness to the invisible illnesses, the ones people know so little about. She does that and more by using her other passion, writing.

23:27 is her debut novel and is the closest to her heart. The issues dealt with in this novel are the kind that touch everyone in one way or another. She hopes that each reader takes something from this book and learns from it.

CPSIA information can be obtained
at www.ICGtesting.com
Printed in the USA
LVOW13*1426150318

569988LV00011B/178/P